VIGNETTES FROM THE LANDED GENTRY

Outlandish Tales
from the Trailer Park

Pandemic Bedtime Stories

RONDI SPRINGER

ISBN: 978-0-578-27231-3 (Paperback)
ISBN: 978-0-578-27230-6 (eBook)

This is a work of fiction loosely based on actual events. All the characters, organizations and events portrayed in this book are either products of the author's imagination or are used fictitiously.

In no way are these stories encouraging derision or making fun of mental illnesses; some of the fictional stories reflect interactions with people who seem to have undiagnosed, unmedicated, or untreated mental illnesses. How else can one explain such outrageous behaviors?

An individual's fundamental right to choose or deny medical care is sacrosanct. When a person is clearly struggling with their mental health but refuses any care or treatment because they are drowning in the symptoms of said mental illness—and there is no one who can force them to receive care—then I don't know how to help.

When or if mental illness overtakes them, and their behaviors reach a dangerous tipping point, then for the safety of others, it's time for them to move on. Mockery was not intended, nor was portraying anyone as the butt of any joke.

What is being relayed, dear reader, are fictional stories loosely based on actual events. Sometimes, even mentally ill people can turn into asshats, much like a lot of the general population, especially during the pandemic.

CONTENTS

CUSTOMER SERVICE— HOW MAY I HATE YOU?

Pre-pandemic, the RV park was an overnight or short-term stay campground. One would rumble in with their fifth wheel or toy hauler in tow, grumble in a motorhome, or pull in with a travel trailer. There are a variety of recreational vehicles and fans of all types.

One would register at the office, pay, receive rules, including bathroom and WIFI codes, and the complimentary bundle of wood for the fire pit at each site.

"Enjoy your stay!" would be said with a smile and a free tide book!

There was no opportunity to learn intricate personal details and alarming mental issues in less than 48 to 72 hours, two weeks, or an unusual month's long stay; one would take any potential crazy with them while leaving their trash, shit, and shower water behind.

It's difficult to explore and share all one's repressive messed up shit if one is only here temporarily. All emotional baggage is packed up when one leaves.

Bad behaviors have been amplified and multiplied since the Great Pandemic began its reign of terror, and it continues to this day. Sadly, it may continue forever.

The lockdown, the isolation, the job loss, and fears have altered the landscape and magnified ugly entitled behavior.

Or maybe there's always been an oversupply of asshats who now believe they have permission to proudly and loudly show their work.

And dude… it's an ugly look.

During the pandemic, the health department ordered the campground to be closed, except for monthlies (those who pay month to month). So, we switched over in order to stay in business and pay the bills. By "we," I mean just me (pluralis majestatis).

The health department finally lifted that restriction (with major limitations), but the campground was already filled with monthlies, and it just felt safer than having people coming in overnight. I don't know where these short-term visitors have been or what they've touched. Remember how scary it was at the onset of Covid days?

Since the pandemic doesn't seem to be ending, we will stay a long-term park until it's safe to do otherwise. At present, we are still in the throes of the pandemic, with variations lurking in every nightmare scenario. My best guess is that there will be many further mutations of this scourge.

Would I make more income as a short-term transient park? Most likely, but I can't see myself putting my life and the health of others in danger when the pandemic is still cruising along. But wait, there's a possible Covid cousin coming along in a couple months that is potentially lethal, well, more lethal?

Seriously, monkeypox in 2022? What's next?

I can't tell if I'm doomscrolling, or is that just a dose of the daily news?

Anyway, the adventures in this book are generated directly from the effects of the pandemic. I now am a landlord, rather than a transient park host.

I thought being a landlord would be a quiet job—maintenance, watering and gardening, sweeping, making sure rent is paid, bills paid, a quiet existence.

Well, that's a fantasy. It's amazing how the most miniscule of complaints have now filled my day.

I must mediate spats and feuds, and I don't know why they are talking to me about it.

Just talk to the person instead of ratting them out!

They parked too close to your site?

They dumped their tank on the wrong day?

They won't pick up their dog poop? Just give them these free doggie bags and tell them to pick it up!

Their music is too loud?

She gave you a mean look. Seriously?

And the list goes on and on and on…

There are days where I am completely worn out by this childish, emotionally draining nonsense.

I've had numerous landlords, and not once did I consider calling them and asking them to settle a dispute or disagreement with any of my neighbors. I can just see how long I'd last if I called and bitched that my neighbor parked in front of my unit, or that another neighbor let their dog poop in my yard or God forbid, a mortal sin, someone's cat sat on my car.

But these people?

A bunch of kids tattling, "Mom, he touched me!"

"Mom! He's on my side!"

"Mom!"

Sigh.

You can thank the pandemic for this book.

Everybody is so butt hurt all the time. I don't get it. Where did all the adults go?

Now onward.

I freely admit that I'm in the wrong profession. I'm not a people person.

I do have a cool job though, and these are the fun parts:

Stop me right there. I hate when I'm looking at a recipe and trying to figure out if I need lemongrass or some other exotic stuff and I'm stuck with a lengthy exposition as to where this recipe came from—(Nana or a trip to Amalfi) and that the chef has been earthing (you look it up) and enjoying goat yoga and that she gave birth at home, ate her placenta, robs banks, kills hitchhikers, is lactose intolerant, composts, and has a great natural remedy for warts. Stop, stop, stop! That is enough of that. Just give me the recipe!

Wait? A natural remedy for warts? Does it involve burying something in the yard under a full moon?

Stop, wait, back to the recipe… I mean story…

I'm not going to bore you with some prolonged explanation as to how I got here. I am not the story; the stories are the stories.

Hopefully, my telling these stories doesn't make me *too much* of an asshat, but let's find out!

Before this introduction transforms into something tortuous you skip to get to the actual recipe (the stories of assholery), I just wanted to say that I am outside every day, I get to hang with my peeps, and it's all good.

Here are several of my colleagues. They lack a work ethic and discipline, but they are great at brainstorming new ideas, especially if it involves breaking into the grain container.

Kids on the playground

Enough about boring me, let's go back to campground fun and games. Everyone! Gather around the campfire! There are stories to tell!

About that campfire, please don't toss your half-empty Aqua Net canister into the fire… that's simply hot shrapnel coming back at ya in about a minute.

If there is a sign at the entrance, and a sign at the driveway, and a placard near the office, all which state no vacancy, do not enter, why do they keep coming in? I had a guy yesterday roll in and said, "I want to make a reservation for two nights in June 2022."

It's September 2021. *Uh, no, I'm sorry. I cannot help you. Who knows what June will look like! The future is terribly uncertain!*

And, by the way, he literally drove past the 8' by 10' bright yellow banner affixed to the fence stating in bold black lettering, "Monthlies only, no overnight RVers." I told him to try the campground up the road.

Oh, excuse me, be right back.

Damn it, okay, I'm back.

Whilst writing this, I had to interrupt contemplation to get in my rubber boots and raincoat and step over numerous sleeping cats to get outside.

These cats are supposed to be catching rodents, but instead, they are lolling about. Talk about having trouble finding good help...

I just chased a woman who drove onto the property with a rusty, creaking minivan with bad suspension and Saran Wrap and duct tape covering the broken windows. That Saran Wrap was clever, DIY windows. I've seen some with Hefty trash bags but those make the interior a bat cave and the ability to look both ways impossible.

She didn't use the main road but was slowly driving up the side road, and I finally got her to stop by cutting through the sites and waylaying her as she drove toward me.

It was very windy and the van looked like it was laboriously breathing with the duct tape and that billowing (clever) Saran Wrap.

With one hand raised like a crossing guard, I gave her the universal sign to roll down her window, fist turning in a circle.

Her driver's window rolled down a couple inches (one of the few with glass intact) and the woman who was either young or old (hard to tell) looked highly put upon.

I asked, out of breath from my sprint, "May I help you?"

She frowned. She was severely unwashed, had grime embedded in her scrawny neck rings, white showing around her skittery eyes, gaunt cheeks, and a righteous sense of indignation.

She's so mad at me for interrupting her meticulously planned outing. Time is of the essence and this delay is costly. The agenda has been disturbed!

"I'm looking for my friend who lives here," she retorted angrily, as if it was none of my business.

Here we go. You know she doesn't know who she's looking for, and she's just biding time for that meth riddled noggin to fabricate a name. I have a sneaking suspicion she's looking for something to steal and add to the van's abundant inventory of junk.

I've stopped guys in pickup trucks, empty beds, asking me if I sell propane and I know they are looking to grab a tank and run since they don't have one with them. These cylinders are in very short supply. You know, the pandemic and all.

My propane tank was stolen from my fifth wheel while I was inside, sound asleep. I woke in the morning freezing because, well…

Back to the unwelcome visitor…

"Who are you looking for?" I ask.

She's frowning, searching for a name, like mentally tossing aside dirty laundry, looking for that one halfway clean shirt with only moderate body odor.

"Um, Jay Jason."

Really?

"No one lives here by that name, please exit the property."

An ordinary response from a normal, sober person would be to peacefully exit the property. She'd been asked to leave, and I'm not going anywhere until she does. Also, I will contact the cops if she doesn't. Does she want to go that far? Oh, but of course. This discourse has been added to her urgent to-do-list. Other vital errands can wait.

Let the Meth Debate begin:

"This is public property," the stranger proclaims.

"Nope, it's private and you are trespassing."

"If my friend lives here, I can come onto the property."

"Again, you are trespassing and if you don't leave immediately, I'm calling the cops."

Thus begins her strident, nonsensical diatribe about how this is public land, and I can't bar her from public property. With a hilarious twist, she says that I'm breaking the law because these are *her* RIGHTS on which I'm infringing. I'm curious—where did she go to law school?

She then continued to yell her legal position as she passed one of many signs posted, "Private property, trespassers will be prosecuted."

On her way off the property, she drove by the large sign at the entrance that stated all visitors must sign in at the office, rolled her driver's window down a bit more, and flipped me off. I hoped that made her feel better.

All this nonsense, for no good reason at all. Sometimes, I wonder what is driving this new universe.

I am tired of chasing people through the campground who are just "looking." You are not allowed to do that. This is for the protection of all who live here and want to let their kids play, leave their doors unlocked, and have their possessions unmolested.

When was the last time you entered a hotel, snuck past the reception desk, went up the elevator and wandered the hallways trying to peek into rooms while the check-in clerk was running after you?

Let's also assume there's a sign outside the hotel, "NO VACANCY, TRESPASSERS WILL BE PROSECUTED," which you passed while driving through the entrance and most likely parked illegally in a handicapped spot because you are an entitled asshat.

It's rude and you bypassed ALL the signs. Okay, enough of that.

Let's return to the stories in this book; these individuals should never have been accepted for long-term tenancy. People who stayed, and then very much *over*stayed their welcome.

These special ones are so egregious, so over the top, that they deserve recognition for their unabashed assholery.

Thus, the book was born, to regale you, my good reader, with outlandish tales from the RV park. As a bonus, and you are forewarned, there will be photos. Some are palate cleansers to break up the melodrama, and others… well, you'll see.

It would be a disservice to describe all the genuinely wonderful, empathetic and caring individuals I've had the honor to meet. Suffice to say, good people outnumber bad 10 to 1. Thank God.

But that one out of ten, let's discuss them. I cannot include all asshats, so I've created an amalgam of RVers and their entertaining antics during the pandemic.

There *are* some stand-alone dumbasses that are the worst sort of unicorn.

I've always believed telling people they are being horrid is a waste of time.

Just saying, if a mother repeatedly allows her child, with no coat or shoes in forty degrees icy rain, to run around for hours on end, will my telling her that's wrong accomplish anything? It would be a waste of time.

The ensuing assholery was orchestrated by the pandemic which led to long-term monthlies, and then to put a cherry on that pandemic pie, there was a state-wide eviction moratorium that began as a reasonable amount of time and then began to stretch and lengthen like the world's worst demonic taffy pull.

That moratorium made it almost impossible to evict asshats, and *they knew it.*

All the world's a stage. This show was performed at a RV park.

I also haven't, and won't, discuss in any detail people that have scared the crap out of me. I'm not going to write about them, or even think about them.

Much like looking into the abyss, that abyss knows where you live and has already scoped out the flimsy lock on your particle board front door, and the dimensions of the doggie door on the back door, thinking they just might fit with a little effort. If not them, then maybe their underfed kid can squeeze through and unlock the front door.

What a frighteningly cold, calculating appraisal…

Let's get off those worrisome scary feelings. I just don't want to go there. *Brrrrrr.*

Onto vignettes from the landed gentry (pretentiously raising arms like Evita on the balcony.)

Enjoy your pandemic bedtime stories. Buckle up.

THAT'S SO METHED UP

Birdy and Fred

Birdy came into the park terminally ill and was under hospice care. She was a very sweet woman, too young to be this mortally unwell. Her son, Fred, was allowed to stay on the property only because she needed twenty-four-hour care. He was also allowed to stay because Birdy loved her boy, and she wanted him with her for comfort.

Fred cared for his mother until the very end. He was a good son, but a bad guy.

Fred, who had a seriously lengthy criminal history, was on parole, which didn't end for a good eight months. His record, spanning numerous years, consisted of over one hundred charges for misdemeanors and felonies. They ranged from identity theft, conspiring to commit a felony, driving with no license, possession of a stolen vehicle, hindering arrest, theft, burglary, criminal mischief, theft of services, possession, distribution, and credit card fraud. He'd been a low-level criminal most of his adult life and had spent more time inside than out.

It was oddly impressive that Fred's learning curve was completely, utterly flat.

Or maybe after the fiftieth arrest, he pragmatically decided a life of crime was his only viable career path. Maybe at that point, he was correct.

If Fred ever went on datingfelons.com, his profile would read: I like to steal cars, identities, possess, deliver meth and commit crimes of opportunity because of my low impulse control. And long walks on the beach at sunset. (Because everyone includes that last bit. Who doesn't like the beach at sunset?)

I told him that if it weren't for his mom, he wouldn't be allowed to live on the property. He promised he would be law abiding. Promises, promises.

The closer his mother got to death's door; the more Fred reverted to his baser nature. Perhaps it was the stress of taking care of his dying mom, or it was just habit.

Other relatives visited in her final days, but her son did the heavy lifting. I cannot fault him for his loving care. I didn't know her well, but she was a nice woman who thankfully had someone to look after her, albeit a guy who dealt drugs and was using. But he was her baby boy, and she needed him during this final process.

Fred was tall, lanky, pasty faced with a slow low drawl. Whenever he got mad or yelled, his ill-fitting dentures would fly out of his mouth. He was pretty good at catching them in mid-air, but pretty good is not great.

The five second rule was made for him.

He started selling his mother's pain pills, or maybe just pills he picked up somewhere. Vehicles driving on the property late at night headed straight to his mom's RV. He shook pills into his palm by the vehicle's headlights. He then would exchange his handful for a wad of cash. These transactions would be hazily recorded on my outdoor video system. I can't stay up 24/7 policing everyone.

I'm used to a lot of bad behavior, and his didn't scare me, especially since I told him if he pissed me off, I would be calling his P.O. That threat seemed to slow him down—not stop him, but just made him put the brakes on his behavior a little.

I wasn't about to call the P.O. until his mother passed; I think Fred relied on my goodwill to get away with a lot more because I was worried about his mother's final days.

We all die alone, but Birdy wanted someone at the end to hold her hand.

My warning regarding the parole officer was an idle threat at that point, like saying, "I'm gonna turn this car around if you guys don't stop fighting," when we're heading to a place I want to go.

Fred didn't stop with the pills, he then graduated to dealing meth at the campground. At that time, I could name four people I was sure were using and they hung out with Fred. Also, I would catch non-tenant pedestrians furtively coming to his door and exiting quickly.

P.S. every one of his customers was evicted as soon as the pandemic moratorium lifted. Such brazen assholery cannot be tolerated. Most of them were very, very surprised.

That eviction moratorium was turning the RV park from a reasonably nice, quiet, peaceful place into a rabid chimpanzee exhibit at the zoo and Fred's drug dealing certainly wasn't helping.

All of this occurred as his mother was being visited daily by hospice nurses. Of course, he knew when the nurses would be there, so most of this activity took place after dark. I never said he was stupid; he was most certainly cunning.

Let me revise that, he was stupid. He not only dealt drugs but used them as well.

Have you ever smelled meth? It's one of those odors that once you identify (like decomposition) you can't forget. That olfactory sense memory, like smelling candy canes and thinking of the holidays, now imagine the smell of meth is what a weeks old zombie would smell like, running full tilt at you, rotting arms outstretched and shrieking, "BRAINS!"

It's a distinctive burning wire/plastic, sweetish, acidic, chemically nauseating smell. The smell is tangible and dangerous; it coats the lungs with an oily, toxic paint and strangles breath.

It smells like it's gleefully anticipating your slow murder.

Fred made friends with his southern neighbor, Kelly, or perhaps they were friends before…and she obviously had been using for several months. She was emaciated, stick-thin, stayed up all night and slept during the day.

She had been a beautiful woman, but meth brutally carved away that attractiveness. She had also been kind, but that wasted away as well and there was a bitter quality to her conversations, just a meth meanness that seeped into her tone of voice.

Fred would drive Kelly into town. At first, I assumed he was helping her with groceries, but then I suspected more nefarious motives were afoot; she was helping him pick up inventory for sale around the area. Kelly's story will be continued later.

Birdy and Fred were here for mere weeks. The sicker Birdy got, the less I saw of her. She had enjoyed sitting at her picnic bench under the apple tree and warm sunshine, watching the hummingbirds. No one cared if you're outside in a bathrobe and slippers, that's your place. I'm glad her final days were peaceful.

Birdy passed in the comfort of her own home, and I gave him a couple weeks to grieve, get her affairs in order, and move out.

Long after those couple weeks passed, I approached his site, knocked on the door and waited, hearing shuffling, rustling, and muffled voices before the door swung open. He held both sides of the doorframe for support. He was clearly impaired. I stated that he was not a tenant, and he was a barely tolerated guest when his mom was the tenant. An ex-tenant, that is. When was he moving out?

Glancing inside the dimly lit RV, I saw two obviously intoxicated addicts lolling about on a sofa covered with fast food wrappers and debris. There were also empty beer cans on the floor. Christ, his mom recently passed, and he'd already trashed the interior.

I gave them two minutes to get off the property or the cops would be called. I stepped aside as they stumbled down the RV steps and moved off the property, mumbling the usual insults and vague threats.

Fred yelled at me, something about invading his privacy, and barely caught his dentures. I didn't hear what he slurred, too interested in his hand-eye coordination, which was remarkable given that he was crazy swaying. What a way to squander a beautiful morning.

He attempted to hand me an application he'd picked up from the front office, I waved it away and told him we'd been over this already. Lifelong felons, and especially active drug dealers, cannot live here. That made him mad, but I didn't care. I didn't need the reputation that this was the place to score drugs. That news would spread like wildfire and most likely had already.

The looming specter of the P.O. kept him in check. I told him to vacate the property, or I'd call the P.O. He did end up leaving after he gathered his belongings and moved to a motel in town.

I paid to pull the RV out of the site; he hadn't paid rent and I didn't want him sneaking back; thus, with no sewer, power, or water, the RV became a cold, dark, musty metal box parked behind the garage.

He returned a few days later and asked me very politely if he could come onto the property to clean up the RV for sale. I agreed, and that the daily storage rate was now $12.00, the rate designed to get his ass in gear. He must also pay the back rent due and the tow fees. Surprisingly, he agreed.

Fred would come on to the property at four in the afternoon (meth/vampire traits) and shamble around the interior for an hour or so, then come out and visit several sites of tenants for drug deals.

Nope, that wasn't happening.

I told him he was not allowed to wander the property; his deal was to clean up the RV and get it gone. He didn't like that. At the rate he was going, that RV would never be ready for sale. And that's what he intended... this was a good gig. A safe place to store drugs, and a safe place to deal drugs at $12.00 a day.

Fred used his dead mother's RV as a warehouse for his meth inventory. I'm surprised Birdy didn't haunt him.

I caught up to him while he was at a tenant's RV, and both Fred and the tenant looked surprised and guilty. I'd deal with *that* tenant later, and told Fred to get off the property or I would call his P.O. As he was leaving, he said, "You can't do that! I'm calling the police!"

Well, guess what? He did call 911 and reported that I had stolen his RV. I marveled at his audacity. What an overinflated sense of entitlement. Or maybe he was just super high.

The cops came and asked me about my kicking him off the property. I explained that he's *not* a tenant, please review his extensive criminal history, he was a guest here only until his mother passed. I also mentioned he was dealing drugs, and I'm pretty sure they were in his mom's RV. Drugs would be safer at the campground than that sketchy motel where he was staying. The cop said if I thought he was dealing drugs, I should call the narcotics line. I said I would.

The cop continued, "Well, he says you're holding onto his RV."

I laughed and said, "He's free to get it off the property, but he's not allowed to wander around. In fact, I want it gone as soon as possible."

The cop replied, "Okay, I'll tell him that." *Like Fred hadn't been told a thousand times already.*

I added, "You can also tell him he can't come back until he pays his storage fees in full." Twelve dollars a day can add up quickly. And theft of services was on his lengthy resume of bad deeds. He had made payments, but these storage fees accrued quickly.

Fred behaved for about three weeks, cleaned up the unit, stayed away from the other tenants, paid his storage fees in full and sold the RV. Maybe someone in authority had a word with him.

There was now no reason for him to enter the property; I'd made it clear that if he stepped onto the property, he'd be charged with trespass.

Just a heads up, during the pandemic, unless it was a serious offense, the miscreant got a warning, and maybe a fine for trespassing. In normal times, if one was charged with criminal trespass, it would mean jail time. But that wasn't true any longer. They couldn't crowd the jails with minor crimes during Covid's reign.

These are pandemic times.

Fred was on parole, but still very hard of learning.

He came back onto the property even after all my warnings, playing his music loudly with his windows open while pulling up to Kelly's RV for a drug mule date.

It was a meth filled vehicle blasting with dead guy rock and roll, much like an ice cream truck with a frenetic jingle to attract the kids.

Yay! The meth man is here! Say goodbye to your teeth!

I called the cops, and they caught him on the property and told him next time, he would be arrested for trespass. I think they also said something about his P.O. would be notified as well, since he was on parole, and this would violate the terms.

From then on, Fred would park at the entrance with windows down to let me enjoy his booming high school prom tunes while Kelly tottered out to either exchange sex for meth or help him move meth. Who knows?

Kelly would complain on the local transit bus that none of her friends were allowed where she lived, and the other methy riders unanimously agreed that the manager was a bitch. This was relayed to me by bus riding tenants *and* the bus driver. More than once. All of them wanted to pass on the local scuttlebutt that a majority of meth heads considered me simply awful.

Geez everyone, thanks for sharing.

I *want* every meth head to know that I'm mean as a snake. I want them to tremble in their unlaced sneakers. There were days it looked very *Dawn of the Dead* (1978) when the meth heads twitched and paced across the road and waited for a pal to emerge since they knew they were not welcome.

Back to Fred the Methman.

I was pretty sure that Kelly was his mule because they would be seen at various motels in the area, him parked, her walking the halls, so I believe he gave her the drugs and she delivered them.

I had called the sheriff's narcotics squad and described Fred, his vehicle, and my suspicions. I then had undercover cops driving through the park, which I appreciated, since it sent the active users scurrying into their RVs.

It was hilarious when noisy Fred pulled up with rock and roll blaring, saw the undercover cops patrolling the campground, and immediately u-turned and sped down a private alley and disappeared, his music's echo chasing him. This confirmed my suspicions of his current career choice—and his vehicle's inventory.

He abandoned Kelly as she slowly shuffled toward the entrance, oblivious to what just occurred.

She'd been stood up.

I saw Fred around town for several months after that. For those one hundred plus felonies and misdemeanors, not one was for a violent crime. Maybe I was lucky for that; Fred never threatened me, he just tried to take advantage of the situation.

I never called his P.O., but I'm sure those two have been in frequent and unpleasant contact after our adventure.

Lastly, when I thought Fred played his music loudly to harass me, it wasn't that at all. I learned that he was severely hard of hearing.

It was very presumptuous of me to assume he was exhibiting bad behavior based on his past bad behavior. My bad.

PALATE CLEANSER

Bunny and Peewee

Kelly

You've met Kelly briefly in the previous story. She lived at the campground for almost a year. Her health got progressively worse. Active meth users don't get better.

I've asked recovering addicts what the attraction is when they know it's so lethal. It's unanimous; meth is wonderful! It is the best feeling in the world! No wonder it is so dangerous. Chasing that ephemeral high is a losing proposition.

God, that was very preachy, my apologies. Of course, the drug must be wonderful despite the dangers, duh. And that's why people like it so much. Well, that and its highly addictive nature. Ah, dopamine.

Among other physical damage, meth punches out your teeth. Feel free to google meth mouth.

Anyhow, Kelly was a very pretty woman, took pains with her appearance, was always courteous, friendly, and had no criminal record. Kelly had been employed, and now was reaching or met retirement age and was unemployed, thus, lots of free time. She had a few gentlemen callers. When they signed in, they were always masked and polite.

Kelly was the type of woman who bought more groceries than she could carry because someone would invariably step in and help her.

I had one altercation with her; she had taken a shopping cart onto the property and left it at another woman's site and said she could have it. Well, that woman didn't want it and tattled on Kelly.

I told Kelly she had brought stolen property onto the campground, and it was her responsibility to return it to the market. Oh, she didn't like my mean mom ways, but she rolled it off the property. I watched her on the highway pushing it in the direction of the market just to ensure she didn't dump it and hightail it back to the park.

Kelly's physical and mental changes were gradual at first, then accelerated, much like skating down a steep hill and realizing there's no way to stop.

I've learned from witnessing meth's stealthy encroachment that it literally shrinks one's perspective and excitement for the future. It makes the world very puny, compressed into simple need.

Already petite, Kelly lost even more weight, and the gentlemen callers tapered off. She approached a couple on the property and asked if they wanted to smoke with her. They declined. She then focused her hungry, longing gaze on the husband, batted her eyelashes, simpered, and girlishly inquired if they were married or if he wanted to help her with some… things. The wife told her to go away, and Kelly retreated to her trailer.

Later, Kelly approached another tenant with a purse full of small baggies filled with meth, an inventory much larger than personal use and asked the tenant if she wanted any. That tenant refused and told me.

Later, but not that much later, events rapidly cascaded.

The paramedics were called, and she was loaded onto an ambulance; she was so intoxicated that she fell asleep on a heating pad for most of a day and it burned her back, resulting in open sores loaded with infection which left her hospitalized for over a week.

Back from the hospital, she was thin and wobbly, her hair still stylishly coiffed.

Her mother and father stopped by with groceries and occasionally drove her from the park to destinations unknown.

I never approached this well-preserved couple in their late seventies to voice my concerns regarding their daughter.

Why? I didn't want to be rude? Geez, I'm rude ALL the time.

And you know what? I didn't have to tell them. They knew. They knew she was an addict. How could they not?

I lazily disregarded the fact that she slept all day, and at night was up disturbing the neighbors. She would go from site to site, knocking on doors and chatting.

Tenants would complain, but in a way that they felt sorry for her. Shamefully, I did nothing.

Kelly, at this point, was a vampire. Wake up, smoke meth, then do it all over again. However, she still managed to make her dates with Fred. Those dates were vital.

She was disruptive, chaotic, and pitiful. She pestered a couple pregnant with twins and declared she was psychic and predicted the death of Fred's mom, Birdy. She woke them at 2 a.m. to impart the news of her magical ability.

Kelly wasn't psychic enough to realize they would tattle on her. She was now working toward an eviction, and she was just about there.

Fred and his mom used to live on the northern side of Kelly's unit. There was a new family living there—three adults, daughter, mother, and the fiancé of the daughter.

I got a call from that site north of her; in the middle of the night, Kelly attempted to break into their RV storage area below the living space.

Fred, living with his terminal mom, kept his drugs in the "basement" of the RV while Birdy was alive. There was no way he had his stash in the living area while she was dying. Fred respected and loved his mom; he wouldn't do that to her.

Kelly, psychotic from lack of sleep and nutrition, crept across her yard and pried at these new folks' "basement" storage area with a tire iron.

Fred is long gone, yet she did not remember in the throes of meth and need. Night after night, she scuttled across her yard, leaned over the locked cabinets under the living area of the RV next to her and attempted to pry them open to find treasure packed in tiny plastic baggies.

I can't tell you how sad that made me.

I can tell you how pissed off those tenants were. They installed a motion light directed at her unit, and that helped; that splash of light seemed to slap her out of her delusion that Fred was still living next to her. Annoyed the neighbors? Sure, but what else could they do?

When she was confronted with the damage to their RV, it was denial and anger. I just had to wait—the lawyer said it wasn't enough for an eviction at that time.

When the pandemic moratorium finally lifted after over a year of extensions, she immediately received an eviction notice. She didn't fight it and quickly found another place to live.

I gave her a decent reference and hoped she would change her ways. Her parents moved the trailer out, and I wished them all the best.

Fred stopped coming around because there was no drug mule to do his dirty work; her other male company had dried up long ago. The dawn of the dead meth heads stopped ambling on the road near the entrance; there was no one left at the park for them to visit.

I heard from several tenants that they had seen her, and she looked healthy and sober. She had a turnaround, hopefully an epiphany that she wanted to live. I was so glad.

A further update: I received a text from her, December 1, 2021. Summarizing her text, she asked me to keep her current address a secret because she was being stalked by a bad guy. I told her no worries and asked if she wanted him arrested for trespass if he did come on the RV park property.

She said no, and I've found the next sentence a common theme when it comes to bullies. Her text read, "I fear if you trespass him outta there he will come back on me somehow."

So that's how bullies operate—they use fear of escalating violence to keep their victims silent.

I texted back and said no one here would tell anyone where she was.

I'm glad she was doing better. Last thing she needed was some degenerate drug addled asshat intruding on her life.

She'd been there, done that.

Chelsea

I accepted the application from Chelsea, a woman in her mid-thirties, with two small girls, approximately two and a half and eighteen months old. Both she and her boyfriend (not the babies' daddy) worked at a fast-food restaurant in town.

From her application, she had been living in her RV on her mother's driveway and needed a place to live.

For the record, when anyone says they've been living in their RV on their mother's driveway, it's a lie. They just don't want to list the places from which they've been evicted.

After dealing with these two, *I have not* and will *never ever ever ever* eat fast food again. The thought of them handling food for human consumption gave me the willies.

Onward with the story… their application was accepted. The family moved in, and during the first couple of weeks, there was a fire in their RV; the fire started when her curtains got too close to the stove's burner.

Thankfully, the next-door neighbor saw the smoke, rushed over with his fire extinguisher, and put out the flames.

She was inside with her children when it happened but didn't even realize there was a fire. The size of an average RV is approximately 300 square feet. How can you not see or smell the smoke billowing out the window (which alerted the neighbor) or hear the smoke alarms? Were the alarms disabled? Were batteries missing?

After that, she apologized and said it wouldn't happen again. Wouldn't happen again? Jesus, it shouldn't have happened once. She was very fortunate the neighbor was home and had a fire extinguisher.

RVs, by their nature, are highly combustible. This could have ended quite badly. RVs are constructed with several toxic chemicals/ VOC (volatile organic compounds): formaldehyde, ethyl alcohol, and others which off gas in the interior, but if there's a fire…

Well, let's just serve up a warm helping of carcinogens straight into panicked lungs.

About three weeks into their stay, besides a load of trash or three, she moved two refrigerators to her front yard. RV refrigerators have special door locks so that when the RV is in motion, those doors stay locked. It would be impossible for a small child inside one to open it once closed. They sat there, doors ajar, so her children, who played unattended in the site, could enjoy a potentially lethal playground created by an unfit mother.

Chelsea was asked several times to remove the refrigerators. Never happened until I did it. Yes, there's trash lying about. This is less than a month into their tenancy. Why? I'm sure her answer would be, "why not?"

During their stay, I noticed there was an increase in activity in the women's restroom early in the morning. It usually happened between 2:00 and 3:00, when the bathroom door was repeatedly slammed shut. Initially, I put it down to the night shift workers at the local smoker, the cheese factory, and the hospital. I was wrong.

My bedroom was less than twenty feet from the women's restroom; thus, I got to hear that slam, slam, slam during those early hours.

I'm working twelve-hour days, getting into my bed at 9:00 p.m. and up at 5:00 a.m., so don't mess with my beauty sleep, bitches. It's obvious I'm not getting enough.

After being awakened *again* by the slammed door, I got up, shuffled into my house slippers, masked and coated, walked over to the women's restroom, unlocked the door and, Christ, really?

Again, this is during the early days of the pandemic where there was no known vaccine, and everything is potentially deadly—doorknobs, toilet seats, sink faucets, air, etc. The pink paint of the restroom stall doors surrounding the handles had literally been corroded away by daily applications of Lysol and bleach.

Chelsea was in the shower area lounging on the wooden changing bench with an unknown homeless looking female, both of whom were fully dressed. A miasma of methamphetamine and cigarette smoke hovered near the ceiling which the fans had trouble removing.

Chelsea's two toddlers, both under three years of age, were barefoot, clad only in low hanging soggy diapers for a night in the low forties. They were fighting for possession of the toilet bowl brush on the public bathroom floor.

Oh my god. I shouted in a panic, "Get that toilet brush away from your kids!" (Covid lingers in poop by the way).

"I thought it was clean!" Chelsea stupidly replied as her 18-month-old wielded the toilet bowl brush like a redneck scepter to hit her older sister full in the face. There were no screams while they tussled as the adults watched them, silent as well.

At 2:30 in the morning…

This was too much for my tired brain; I couldn't process this surreal early morning tableau.

It was the worst manger scene ever.

First things first. "You," to the unidentified homeless woman, "Get out. You are trespassing, and I'm calling the cops."

Gathering her plastic bags of belongings, she scurried out and hustled to the entrance; she'd hidden her car along the side of the road and had crept onto the property, obviously by Chelsea's invitation.

The bathrooms were all code locked, so now I'd have to change the code. If not, every meth head or homeless would now know where to take a shit and shower or just a warm place to smoke meth. News will get around shortly. It's amazing how fast meth news travels.

Back to the fun and games in the restroom… "You," to the crack-head mother of two unfortunate children, "Get your children out of here and get back to your trailer."

Chelsea roughly yanked the toilet bowl brush from the girls, and now they started to cry. She tossed it in the general direction of the toilet stalls, thanks very much.

She mewled some nonsense over the noise of her toddlers' tantrum about how her friend needed a shower because she was homeless. She didn't comprehend that this was *not* a homeless shelter, not to mention any remark about the clouds of meth floating above our heads, or the fact that her two kids were covered in bacteria from sitting on the floor of a public restroom playing with the obviously used toilet bowl brush. There were no apologies given regarding the late hour, or just the general inappropriateness of it all.

Also, the homeless woman wasn't taking a shower! They were using the women's restroom as a hotbox for meth! That's it! With her kids in there! Aaaack!

After what seemed like hours of meth debate, I got her out of the restroom and told her she was not allowed to use it any longer. Boy, that pissed her off. It certainly did not stop her from continuing to go into the restroom to smoke drugs, that is, until I changed the women's bathroom entry lock numbers and told the other tenants to not give it to her.

That should do it. Not.

I caught her in the men's restroom, so I had to change that lock code too. I told everyone not to give her the code.

What is it with her and public restrooms? Well, I learned straight from the horse's mouth…

Chelsea argued that she didn't want to do meth in her trailer because it was small, and the kids were in there. So, to her curdled mind, it was logical to take those two kids—because she's a good mom and doesn't leave them alone in the trailer—with her while she smoked meth with a homeless gal pal in the women's restroom in the middle of the night.

Quality family time.

That conversation made me feel like I was losing my freaking mind.

This all took place at the height of the pandemic, long before a vaccine was available.

Every single page of this book should have the heading:

WE ARE IN THE MIDST OF A DEADLY PANDEMIC WITH NO END IN SIGHT AND NO ONE IS PAYING ATTENTION!!!!!

Keeping that in mind makes this behavior even more fantastic.

As I've said before, evictions became super difficult during the pandemic due to the eviction moratorium, and these idiots had now been at the campground for a month, maybe five weeks. All this disturbing behavior occurred in such a brief period.

It didn't take long before more homeless methers were creeping onto the property at her obvious invitation, and belongings were going missing from other sites. She was still attempting to smoke meth at every opportunity, and those refrigerators were still in her yard!

Done, I'm done. I thought about how to get her off the property. Okay, I'm not above extortion.

I emailed her, listed her bad behavior, and stated she had two choices: She could stay here, but I would call her employer and report her and her boyfriend for illegal drug use and that they should be tested immediately. I also would call Child Protective Service and she would, most assuredly, lose her kids.

Or... they could leave.

They packed up the next day and pulled out, leaving the discarded refrigerators and other detritus. Again, owing rent, because that's how these people roll. At least they rolled out...

Such pleasant mementos from crack land!

A couple weeks later, I got a call from a local RV park. The manager and I were acquainted; in the past as a professional courtesy, I'd sent her my standard eviction notice. She began the conversation regarding Chelsea, who had moved into her park.

I reminded the manager to call me before she accepted anyone; she agreed and wished she'd known but Chelsea had told her she had been living in the RV on her mother's driveway. Oh yeah, there's that.

I regaled her with my Chelsea story. The manager said that she found drug paraphernalia in the women's shower area after Chelsea exited the building. What should she do?

Sigh.

I told her to keep it, and call Child Protective Services, which is something I should have done instead of using it as blackmail to get her off the property.

I should have predicted this... getting them gone didn't make anything go away.

I learned later that her children had been taken by CPS; maybe I'm cynical, but those kids, even at that tender age, had most likely been permanently scarred and my extortion to get Chelsea gone didn't affect them.

I'm lying. I should have made that call, even two more weeks in that insufferable household must have been torture.

That was my bad, and I still think about them and hope she doesn't get them back. At least not until she quits drugs. Maybe not even then… She needs to regain her sobriety and love for her children first.

The stuff I witnessed in the middle of the night was awful. She had twenty-three hours of that day left to screw them up and every day after that.

Please remember the refrigerators open and inviting in the front yard. Her children were only two out of a couple dozen at the park. She didn't care about anything but meth.

I'm not excusing the baby daddies; they should have been concerned about the welfare of their daughters, yet not one father came to visit. So, bad dads, truly. You are the problem as well.

DUDE, YOU LIED

I had a single guy come into the park. His application checked out fine and he moved in. A week later, there was a homeless woman at his site. The usual debris-filled car was parked crookedly, tearing up the lawn because it was not on the gravel driveway. How hard is it to color inside the lines? I caught her leaving mid-morning and told her she was required to sign in at the office, and that every night's stay was an extra $10.00.

She stared at me, mouth open, while I was talking, then interrupted. "Can I split wood? Can I fill in the potholes?"

I just looked at her. *Did you hear anything I said?*

"No," I replied, and shook my head, "No."

She drove away, and then I thought about it… yeah, no. There was a reason he didn't include her on the application, like, uh, meth? Felonies? Meth felonies? And now he wanted her as a guest? Was that his plan from the get-go to get around the application process?

I emailed him that she was not on the contract, and that if she was a guest, she must check in and pay the fee. I also added that if he wanted to add her to the application, she wouldn't be accepted if she had a criminal record. I didn't get an answer, which was, well… an answer.

That same night, at 8:00, after I've already worked twelve hours, I saw her drive up the wrong way on the side road, lights off, staying off the main entrance. Seriously? I pulled on rubber boots, shrugged a jacket over my pajamas, and nabbed my flashlight and keys/pepper spray.

I clomped up the road and admired the twinkling mini-lights I put up on the fruit trees that day and got to his door. I knocked,

knocked, knocked, KNOCKED again, and he finally got off his couch and walked to the door. I watched him through his uncurtained, smudged windows thinking, *dude, I can see you.. What is the holdup? You think you have drapes?*

I explained the issue and the email, and he said he didn't read the email. I told him to do so and that she didn't sign in and was told this earlier.

She crept out of the back door of the RV and approached me. She said she didn't know where to sign in (even though I told her that morning). I said, "I'll walk you down," and told him it's an extra $10.00 a night. He made no move to open his wallet.

As we were walking down to the office, she became super confrontational and hyper talkative, and right there I knew it was drugs.

That meth mouth was moving a mile a minute but made very little sense. Her tone went from petulant obsequiousness to outright outrage. She was winding herself up for a fight as we walked the main road past lighted RV's. All was quiet, save for her rising voice.

The argument erupted from her in a spew of hostility. "I forgot to sign in because I didn't know where to sign in, and stop saying I don't live here, I can live here, he said I could."

I quietly interrupted, "You are not on the lease."

She continued rapidly, her voice getting louder with each step as we passed darkened RVs with few lights on. "He said I could, and he can do it because he lives here and I don't know why you don't like me. Why don't you like me, you don't know me, you…"

And right about then, I lost my temper. Why in the world was she trying to pick a fight with me?

I stopped in the lane, and turned to her, my tone calm but firm, "Okay. Enough out of you. On second thought, based on your current behavior, you are not welcome here at all, and you will exit the property immediately." I turned and walked away.

She spun back to the RV, and I went to the house, where I emailed him again and asked him to escort her from the property. He emailed back that she was gathering her belongings and leaving. I emailed a thank you.

This confrontation was at 8:20 p.m., and it took her until 9:45 p.m. to exit—geez, she really did move in. I watched her drive off, then went back to check emails one more time before bed. It was already way past my bedtime.

He had emailed that she had nowhere else to stay, and she had medical issues.

Do you have any idea how much I don't care?

I wrote back stating she was not on the lease and based on her behavior—including sneaking onto the property, not signing in and then becoming highly aggressive with me—she was now banned from the property.

He wrote back saying she didn't sneak onto the property.

Okay, dude, when someone who doesn't live here drove onto the property with no headlights on, went the wrong way up a side road, and avoided signing in, that's sneaky.

But whatever, you're missing the point.

I emailed him back and asked him to confirm that he understood that she was banned from the property, and if he wanted to live with his "loved one" (his words in an earlier email), he could find another place to live—with her. I asked him to let me know if he would be leaving.

He emailed me back saying that I'm mean.

I didn't reply to the mean comment. Frankly, what grown ass adult male used language like that? I'm not your mother. You can't hurt my feelings.

Here's the thing and I'm sure you can see it: He neglected to include his "loved one" on the application because the application would have been rejected. Thus, *his* sneaky behavior. And seriously, I now think she's been here for a longer time than I realized, probably from day one.

He was here since January 16th. It was now the morning of January 30th. That almost set a record for how fast one can screw up. Almost.

Depending on his response to the "do you understand she's not welcome" email, there would be an eviction notice filed shortly.

He responded to my email by emailing me a law and stated that I couldn't stop him from having guests. The law he cited was put in place during the pandemic. It was designed for people suffering from joblessness and threatened with homelessness so that they could move into an apartment with friends or family to ensure a roof over their heads and was a method to slow down transmission of Covid-19.

This had nothing to do with sneaking around the application process.

Also, the law did not make the individual a tenant, just a visitor, and the contract he signed stated that management had veto power over guests.

I didn't need this shit; I had a waiting list.

The attorney drew up the eviction papers and he was served. He had thirty-five days to move out.

A couple days later, a tenant came by to tell me he saw the dude in his truck at one in the morning. The dude wore a miner's light and meth flailed about the interior of his truck, tossing papers aside, searching for hours.

Meth flailing is exactly how it sounds. Imagine someone cranked up on speed and frantically searching for that one receipt in piles of trash. The receipt doesn't even exist. Fevered futility in the wee hours of the morning.

I told him the dude was evicted, and it's only a matter of time before he's gone. I also told him to call the cops if it happened again; maybe I can get him out earlier than the eviction notice by an arrest instead.

The tenant and I did spend a moment wondering where he got that miner's light. Curious, but meth motives are beyond me.

Grossly, the dude added a couple dozen ruined semi-truck tires, none of which fit his truck or RV, to the assortment of shit on that site. Where was he finding all this garbage?

And when I said shit in his yard, besides the trash, I mean actual shit. He didn't pick up his large dog's poops. It was amazing, in a creepy way, how he'd successfully created a pigsty in a matter of days. The dude feathered his nest with cigarette butts, random hubcaps, empty bottles, and lumber too big for the fire ring. A meth mosaic.

Maybe now it felt like home.

To add insult to injury, he towed a clearly self- constructed trailer onto the property. It was a trailer frame, but wooden slats were clumsily affixed to the sides. It looked like something an angry mob would hastily assemble to drive a witch to the stake.

I emailed him and told him to remove it immediately, or I would. The RV sites were not engineered for an additional witch cart, and it dug grooves into the wet grass half in, half out of his site, and partially blocked the road.

He emailed back that I was hindering his ability to work because this was his work equipment. I forgot to mention he was "self-employed."

I emailed him again and asked him to review the signed rental contract. No work equipment was permitted on the property. I repeated that the clock was ticking on its removal.

All of this took place *after* service of the eviction notice.

The witch cart was removed that day, lord knows what street he parked it on, what poor resident woke up to *that* outside their window.

Finally, days after the final move out date, he was gone. He took all that garbage with him, so it must have had some value to him. I spent hours cleaning up weeks of dog poop and random leftover trash and was happy doing so.

He never did pay rent (or the guest fee) while he was here; he was never planning on paying rent at all… such a nice dude. I filed a small claims suit against him even though I figured I'd never see a dime.

He never replied to the small claim summons and complaint, so I won the court case by default. I took the money judgment signed by the judge, forwarded it to a company that chased down deadbeats and they garnished his bank account.

That was successful. I didn't expect his account to have the entire amount due under the writ of garnishment.

I received a call from the dude who screamed that I stole his money. That somehow, he alleged, I got his debit card and stole his money. I listened to him rant and shriek for a good thirty seconds until he slowed, breathing hard and said, "You never paid rent, you stole from me, dude, and I got a writ of garnishment against you for court costs and the rent due."

Well, that set him off, he wasn't a thief, I'm the thief, I stole his debit card (again with that debit card) and I interrupted him, "If you think I stole your debit card, please contact the sheriff's office immediately."

"THIS IS A CIVIL MATTER!" he shouted at me, and I knew that he knew he was in the wrong and he'd already called the Sheriff's office and that's what they told him. He was just pissed off that I outsmarted him.

"Yes, yes, it was a civil matter, and you neglected to reply to the complaint, and the judge granted the garnishment," I replied and ended the call. I waited for him to call back to continue his rant, but surprisingly, he did not.

What do you think about a national registry of asshats? Is that possible? We could have a list of nasty people and their assholery summarized who are totally outside the boundaries when it comes to normal human behavior. It certainly would save me a ton in attorney's fees and time if I had reference material besides the standard background checks. Background checks don't foretell witch carts.

Ironically, I'm pretty sure I'd be repeatedly nominated by all the asshats I've evicted. I had one nasty Yelp review by a woman who complained I wouldn't let her, and her friends, stay for free because she's homeless.

I argued with Yelp they shouldn't allow people to review businesses they *don't* actually patronize, but I didn't get far.

YOU CAN'T WHORE HERE

I got a call from a local agency that assisted abused women find a safe place to live. They had a woman, let's call her Ms. Hooker, who was a domestic abuse survivor and needed a safe place to live.

She filled out the application and would be living alone—which was a *mandatory* requirement of the agency agreement. No other individual was allowed to be in the RV while she was recovering. This rule was designed to keep her away from any bad influences.

This agency would pay her rent for several months to help her get on her feet. I signed all the agency paperwork and met the woman. She seemed okay, just a little too eager to play the victim.

This domestic abuse survivor, before long, was inviting men onto the property, and I mean it was raining men. I told her this was not allowed by me or by the agency paying her rent. She countered with they were just staying for a little bit but wouldn't spend the night.

What part of Covid-19 do you not understand?

I told her we are in a pandemic, and strangers were not allowed on the property. She ignored me. The agency was of no help in getting her to obey its own rules.

Before long, she had set up an inflatable hot tub, in February, where the high was 38 and the low was 26 as she vainly attempted to use all the electricity in the world to heat it to 92 degrees.

I can't turn my back for a second, seriously.

I unplugged it and knocked on her door. I told her to drain the water into the bushes, not into the septic system. Hot tubs were not allowed. She was dressed in a summer halter top, no bra, frayed jeans shorts and bare feet. Can't wait to see the electricity bill this February…

She could hardly hear me over the bass and thump of her rock and roll that poured through the open door. There was a vehicle parked on her site. It was odd since she didn't drive and took public transportation…Oh.

Since these low rent suitors continued onto the property at all hours, I stopped these gentlemen and turned them away at the entrance. Just what I wanted, more work. I was getting bored doing chores twelve hours a day.

Idle hands, you know?

As I was now hall monitor, I accosted a sketchy woman with a ratty backpack who attempted to enter the restroom—a restroom *only* for tenants, not for guests (trying to limit the Covid exposure for the tenants). I asked her who she was.

She said, "My mom lives here, and I just got out of jail for theft." Her mom was the supposed domestic abuse survivor who had snuck her criminal daughter onto the property and who had been hiding her in her RV. I told her the restroom was for tenants only, and she was not allowed. She shrugged and walked back up the road to her mother's RV, and completely ignored my instructions to leave the property.

Again, the conditions of Ms. Hooker's rental agreement mandated she lived alone to provide her time to get on her feet, get a job, and move forward in a positive manner.

Well, she couldn't wait to invite all her bad decisions along for the ride.

Her application didn't list this convict daughter as a relative. You know why? Because I would have researched her and found her on the county inmate jail roster and denied her mother's entrance to the park. The mother argued with me that her daughter could stay.

Her sole argument was repeated in a whiny mewl, "But it's my daughter!"

I called the agency and got no response for a good two weeks. During those two weeks, I chased johns away from the park and tried to get the felon daughter out of the RV. Turns out under the law, if the felon daughter is inside the tenant's RV it's not trespassing.

I swore I would never, ever, ever again do any business with this agency. Maybe this woman was an abuse survivor, but her current behavior wasn't going to help her move forward. She wasn't looking for work to support herself; she was just whoring it up—which was not an approved side gig during a worldwide pandemic at the campground—and now had a criminal on the property who was recently released from a crowded jail. A daughter who was arrested for theft (and heroin possession) was now running around the campground, most likely window shopping.

It frosted me that the Health Department had closed the RV park to transient visitors, and yet that's *all* this woman was having.

This entire episode made my OCD go off the charts; if she had Covid, she was literally patient zero for a massive spread of a fatal virus and no one seemed to care but me. Think about it, if she had the virus, those men she serviced were going home to unsuspecting families, co-workers and friends. It made my skin crawl.

When the agency woman finally emailed me, she said they switched email servers and never got any of my emails. I emailed and asked her if they switched phones as well, because she hadn't returned any of my numerous calls. Stop bullshitting me.

Finally, *finally*, the agency woman called me back and I told her how disappointed I was with her. This tenant must leave immediately. It took a good two weeks to get the tenant and her criminal daughter off the property. Yes, the attorney had to file an eviction notice against her to get this ball moving. Yes, more attorney's fees for trying to do a good deed.

Then, get this—the agency said I must refund the deposit in my possession. I told the agency woman, "Sure, I'll refund ¼ of the deposit to the tenant. The rest is going to the visitor fees for the unauthorized guests at $10.00 a day, and the electrical usage of attempting to heat a jacuzzi in February, and the overuse of water."

She said that it was simply unfair, and the woman should get her entire deposit back. I reminded her she allowed a sex worker to set up shop on my property, her thieving daughter trespassed for weeks, and I had to serve her with an eviction notice. Based on all of the above, the agency could stuff it.

There was radio silence for days. The agency woman finally emailed me and said to send the partial refund to the woman's new address.

I doubted Ms. Hooker stayed there very long because the refund check I mailed had never been cashed.

I was pretty sure that woman continued to behave as she pleased and got removed from that new place as well. Abuse survivor? I feel for true victims of abuse, but this woman scammed both the agency and me and I prayed that she didn't have Covid.

PALATE CLEANSER

Nature walk

EXCUSE ME?

Here are some random thoughts from tenants and bizarre acts from strangers which have caught me completely off guard.

A high wind warning was in effect. The lights were flickering, south winds 40 to 50 mph with 70 mph gusts, rain was already an inch by 10 a.m. and a tenant texted me, swear to God, "What's up with the internet?"

I didn't realize I controlled the weather but let me get right on that. I texted back, hoping it sounded like a neutral reply, not boiling with irritation, "Did you look outside?"

I don't know how to google. That was the response of a tenant when I told them to go online to order an item.

An officer, called on a disturbance of the peace, vest camera on, asked, "Is she batshit crazy?" *Yessir, yessir she is.*

Bike guy, who doesn't live here but wouldn't leave. I warned him I would call the cops to get him off private property. He said he'd wait. So, he did for about forty minutes after I made the call. Seriously… he wouldn't leave until he got a police escort. Once the cop arrived, he biked off the property. The cop looked at me, and I just shrugged. Go figure.

I told a guy who pulled in with a truck and a camper shell that the park's full, no vacancy, but he simply wouldn't leave. He waited around 45 minutes for the cops to escort him off the property. Pissed me off because I had chores to do and didn't enjoy watching him on camera.

Just to be safe, I wasn't going outside to do chores or be confronted. Frankly, when an unknown asshat cranked up the rudeness, I realized they truly don't give a shit about anything. Aggressiveness from a stranger who doesn't get his way is mind boggling and scary. If the park is full, no vacancy, why is that a personal affront? How does that enrage a person?

Some guys just have that "you're not the boss of me" mentality. Cops show up, tell him to leave, he promptly left. What did that accomplish? Did it help his self-esteem?

Speaking of Bike Guy, and the subsequent Truck with a Camper Shell Guy, there's something about a woman telling a guy what he can't do that simply infuriates them. Is it because they are reminded of a nagging mother? Does it make them feel small? Powerless?

I'd bet five bucks if I were a guy built like Thor, they would have left the property immediately, no trouble at all.

But no, since it's me, I must call the authorities to escort these mommy issue men off my land. Mommy Issue Man, MIM. I like it. Maybe I'll get a t-shirt made.

A woman evicted for not paying rent has been running around town stating that I evicted her for sleeping with "my man." I evicted her out of jealousy, and *not* the fact that she'd stopped paying rent and began begging the surrounding tenants for money.

There was a culvert on the road outside the campground that swallowed numerous impaired drivers. I've named it drunk ditch. Seemed appropriate.

Drunk ditch snared a lot of guys.

Mason, a tenant, drove into drunk ditch after day drinking with Kelly.

He wasn't evicted for that, but for harboring homeless people in his RV. He had the gall to tell me he was their AA "sponsor." Don't you have to be sober for that? He never changed his mailing address even after a couple years. Did he not want his stimulus check?

Two scruffy lumberjacks—unshaven, dirty t-shirts, suspenders, in a smoking diesel truck—pulled in and the younger jumped from the passenger side and immediately ran up to the camp host's two beautiful German shepherds on their leads and began to howl and bark at them, winding them up into a frenzy. I watched from the open office door while his bearded pal chortled at the shenanigans. Finally, they realized I was standing there.

"May I help you?" I shouted. The fat ass behind the wheel, while his shit friend was still teasing the dogs, yelled from his open window, "Do you have any sites for monthly rent?" I could hardly hear him over the angry dogs, idling truck, and that barking turd of a lumberjack.

I looked at him. "Yes, I do." Waited a beat and said loudly, "But not for you."

He turned crimson, and I could see he was seriously contemplating getting out of his truck to teach me a lesson.

What a MIM (Mommy Issue Man).

I'm going to make it a thing, like "That's so fetch" (*Mean Girls*).

By that time, the camp host had both angry dogs on leash, and you could tell those highly intelligent and vastly annoyed dogs really wanted five minutes alone with the barking oaf in suspenders who thought he was so funny. They would love to show him funny.

I calmly said, "Get off the property. You're trespassing, disturbing the peace and I'm ready to call 911." My cell was in my hand, and I'd already taken a photo of both knuckleheads and their license plate.

(My cell's photo library is so freaking weird. I get murdered, those poor detectives will have their work cut out for them.)

Thank God the puce faced incipient heart attack driving the diesel realized this would end badly for him and his idiot sidekick. He waved the turd back to the truck and reversed out of the entrance, muttering threats. Good riddance…

Can one imagine those two living here? Oh god, no.

A Hummer sped into the parking area and slammed to a stop, spewing gravel. Guy got out in a hurry and yelled at me over the hood, "Do you sell toilet water?" I shook my head no, and he quickly jumped back into the Hummer, like he was late delivering a donor kidney and rushed away. After he left, I realized he probably meant non-potable water? Not sure. But the answer was no. And why was it a matter of life and death? So confused…

I've just been evicted and need a place. Can I sleep in my car here?

My RV doesn't leak when it doesn't rain. This pithy excuse was generated by my complaining to a tenant that he cannot cover his RV in blue tarp with bungee cords for months on end. He needed to get it fixed and not tell me it worked fine when it didn't rain.

A cordless hole puncher… is a gun.

My brother is going to turn my trailer (18') into a tiny home. But isn't it?

Just a question or two to the dude who left his shit filled boxer shorts behind the toilet. Why couldn't you just put them in the trash? Did you think they wouldn't be found? Were you going to come back later and retrieve them? That was the worst treasure hunt ever.

During the pandemic, the Health Department required that we keep track of visitors into the park—but that's always been my requirement. For the Health Department, it was so they could contact the trace in case of any Covid infection. For me, no one was allowed on the property unless they signed in for the safety of all. This person was told to sign in, and instead left a message about freedom with a vaguely Qanon flavor at the front counter with no addressee. Why is signing in to a private campground a violation of one's freedom?

Hello, Merry x-mas to you and your pet(?) I was in the neighborhood and thought I'd say hello, was advised by your Landlord, I can't be here, ect (sic)—without Signing In?!? NO Thanks, Enjoy your Freedom.

How are you getting eggs, you don't have a rooster.

Homeless guy living in his van came back to the van and the steering wheel was stolen. I laughed when I heard. I'm going to hell.

A guy became very confrontational when I said his application has been denied. He wanted six adults in an 18' RV. I told him it would be the same cost as renting an apartment so he should do that instead (also, I know it would be more than six adults, more like a freaking revolving door of people.) He then gave me a sour look, squinted and said, "So you're not renting to me because I'm Native American?"

I reviewed the rental application in my hand and replied. "No, sir, it's because you're 55 years old and have zero rental history on the application and you've been living in your RV on your mother's driveway."

Again, with the mother's driveway. That's another t-shirt, "My RV's In Mom's Driveway."

"Sir, you need a mask to enter." The gentleman pointed to my face, "Can I borrow yours?"

So glad about my felony, no jury duty for me!

My toilet won't drain, nothing's coming out from the black tank, so I brought the water hose inside and filled it, but now it's gonna overflow. What should I doooooooooooooooooo?

A tenant related that she saw a creepy guy with a flashlight go through the campground on a bike at three in the morning. She told me two days after it happened. I asked her, "Did you call the cops?"

"No," she said. I then explained to her that telling me doesn't do anyone any good. Why do I have to continue to explain this? See something weird? Don't call me, call the cops. And please don't alert me days later. She was the second one to do so about this creepy bike guy.

The soap dispenser in the men's restroom has been filled twice during the pandemic beginning early 2020. *Twice.* Oh, pardon me, just refilled the half-empty bottle, in late 2021. On my way out, I generously Lysoled the doorknob.

I called the sheriff; he promised to drive through the park late at night. Some knucklehead had been sneaking onto the property and siphoned gas from cars and snuck out on foot. A gallon of gas is about 8 lbs. One gallon. FYI, McDonald's in town is starting at $15.00 an hour.

CRACKHEAD PHONE TREE

Sadie moved in with her mother's help, and she lived here for several months. She was in her late thirties and mildly developmentally disabled with the mindset of a fourteen-year-old. Let's all remember what we wanted to do at age fourteen... run around with friends and have fun!

People eagerly took advantage of her sweet naïveté. She lived alone, with an occasional boyfriend, but those didn't work out well. I liked one of them very much, and he helped with yard work. He was also an effective deterrent from the myriad of strung-out meth cockroaches who attempted to scurry onto the property and to her RV. Things quieted down while he was here. He knew the dangers of meth, and rehab worked for him.

But, and there's *always* a but, he was arrested for enticement of a minor for sexual acts, and I felt betrayed and stupid. It's a bad feeling to like somebody and then find out they're corrupt.

Sadie was heartbroken because he was good to her. There were lots of brutal men out there waiting to take advantage of a lonely girl. Wait, didn't I just say he was arrested for attempting to entice a minor for sexual purposes? Damn, damn...

Sadie ran with methy people because it was hard to make friends, and these guys wanted to hang out with her, yay! These newfound friends wanted to come over to her house to party! But guess what? You can't do illegal drugs in the campground! Sadie was terribly lonesome and happily accepted anyone who showed any interest in being a friend.

These sketchy people would attempt to drive or walk onto the property, and when asked where they were going, they would answer, "My friend's house." Oh, no you're not.

It got so bad that these meth heads would knock on the wrong door at 4:00 in the morning.

I turned away half a dozen cars a day filled with two to three individuals. The interiors of the cars were filled with the detritus of wasted lives. The usual convo went like this:

Me: "Hey, hey, stop. Where are you going?"

Super skinny toothless guy who could be twenty or sixty: "My girlfriend's house."

Me: "Where does she live?"

And I swear every time they would vaguely point up the road.

Me: "What's her name?"

He would glance around at the car's interior at his meth addled pals, hoping they could pony up a name. Nope. Couldn't even make that miniscule effort. Evidently, she wasn't worth the time. She was just someone with a place to hang and do drugs, priceless.

Me: "You have a minute to back outta here before I call the cops and have you arrested for trespass."

Sometimes, one of the bolder ones with authority issues would argue with me. They'd say something like, "Who do you think you are? You cunt."

If I had a nickel for every time that word got thrown at me, I'd have approximately $19.35.

My response: "I said to leave (click of my phone taking a photo of their license plate), and now I'm calling 911. You are trespassing and refused to leave."

It was amusing to watch these supposed "friends" leave while yelling out the windows about how I was violating their rights and they would call the cops because it's still 'merica. Yet they exited because one would suspect there are drugs in that vehicle and that they are surely well known to the local constabulary.

I've never seen an active tweaker drive anything other than a crap car, windows that don't roll up the whole way, and spidered cracks in the front windshield. The ceiling upholstery was ALWAYS tattered, like someone in the throes of a three-day insomniac binge propelled by methamphetamine got super dissociative and thought the drugs were hidden in some secret ceiling compartment and it would be a capital idea to tear the interior apart.

In a meth head's vehicle, there's a preponderance of debris, a diorama that just screams, "Look, look at my bad choices!"

A mobile time capsule of a wasted life.

Also, these meth heads would creep around at night looking for things to steal, so everyone was on edge and double-checked to make sure their cars and tools were locked up. This must stop.

Sadie was told she had to tell these "friends" they are not welcome on the property. She pleaded, "But I dooooooo!"

Okay, well, I had trouble believing that and contacted her mother. The options were as follows: either a time out for Sadie to reset her mindset regarding these friends, or I could simply evict her.

I couldn't evict her during the pandemic moratorium, but I took a chance that the mom would support my decision.

The mom agreed with me that Sadie should have a time out from the campground, to think about why she was being removed. Her RV would stay, and she would go live with her mom for a couple weeks.

Let me side-step and talk about Sadie's mom. She was, I believed, a genuinely nice woman. She was not the sharpest knife in the drawer, but she cared about her daughter's welfare. She seemed appreciative regarding my constant vigilance in keeping bad people away from Sadie.

In hindsight, I now know Sadie had welcomed them. But at that point, I was angered that these sketchy meth addicts thought they could run roughshod over Sadie.

Sadie's mom effusively thanked me. I said Sadie must understand that this was it—no more visitors, no more drama, and she could return.

We both agreed that this was the last chance, that if there was another incident, Sadie's mom would remove her from the park.

We had an agreement.

Sadie's mom took her off property for those two weeks, and the place immediately calmed; thus, proving how effectively the crack-head phone tree ran.

Those two weeks quietly flew by, and when Sadie returned, she seemed to understand that this was her last chance.

But remember, she is a teenager and the threats of two weeks ago fade quickly.

She did have a new boyfriend move in, which I vetted. He seemed okay, on the spectrum, perhaps Asperger's, but I'm no expert and it doesn't matter.

He would repeat the same sentences: "I'm only here for a short while. I'm moving back to Idaho." He was gentle with her and had a job. All of that was fine for a few weeks.

It might seem strange to measure relationships in mere weeks, hope springs eternal that this will all work out and they live happily ever after. As if.

He lost his job and sulked in her RV while she gadded about. He became abusive and commanded her daily to walk down and bring back beer from the market two miles away. He was mooching off her, and then events took a turn for the worse.

In the aftermath, when I spoke with her mother, we both agreed this was a proud moment in Sadie's emotional evolution. The boyfriend punched her for some perceived insult, and she kicked him out rather than merely enduring the assault.

Sadie came to me with a bag of his belongings and said they broke up, but he forgot his stuff.

I told her she had every right to evict him and to leave his stuff by the entrance. She should text him to retrieve his belongings. He would not be allowed back on the property.

He never showed up, and what was left after roadside scavengers got through with his belongings went in the dumpster.

After the abusive boyfriend was removed, I noticed Sadie was leaving the RV park at 1:00-2:00 in the morning. (I saw this all on the cameras the next day.)

There was nothing open in town at those late witching hours, so I knew things would be shortly going south. Nothing good happens after midnight.

In the next few weeks, the paramedics showed up at Sadie's RV several times. She had a rapid heartbeat and was scared. It turned out she was using something—not at the campground. She returned, and then had bad symptoms/reactions from the drug use.

I'm a slow learner and figured the paramedics were there for anxiety attacks. I'm an idiot.

Of course, now that the abusive boyfriend was gone, once again, the crack phone tree went on speed dial. I cannot continue spending hours a day chasing down people trying to locate Sadie's trailer so that they can come in, use the facilities, and get high in a nice, comfortable, and safe place.

Meth mooches.

I called Sadie's mother and said my goodwill was used up. I cannot continue to protect her daughter because it was too much work and put everyone at the campground at risk. Sadie's mother said she was out of town camping and would come over on Tuesday and get Sadie and the trailer out of there. I would see her on Tuesday, thank you.

I didn't talk to Sadie about this because what would be the point? Denial? Protestations? Tears?

She wasn't a grownup, and she didn't drive, so who would move her out? Her parents.

Tuesday rolled around, but no Sadie's mother. I called, no response. I left a phone message.

Thursday rolled around, and still no response from Sadie's mom. What the hell? I thought we were on the same page.

Sadie walked onto the property, and I asked, "Sadie, has your mom told you when she's moving you out?"

Sadie stopped, "Why? What?" Her face crumpled and she looked very young.

"We've talked about this; you cannot do meth."

"But I didn't do it here!" she insisted.

I said, "But the paramedics show up here, and you're using."

I didn't bother explaining that the meth phone tree was once again up and running.

Sadie stormed off, her face twisted with shock and dismay. I realized then that Sadie's mom had deliberately chosen to leave her daughter in the dark and had abdicated all responsibility for what would happen next.

What happened next was Sadie called her counselor, she was suicidal, did not want to leave the park, and didn't know that doing meth off property violated the rules.

Her counselor told me that. That yes, Sadie knew drug use on the property was forbidden, that's why she did it elsewhere and came home tweaked. This was her home. She's happy here, and no, no, no, she did nothing wrong.

Next thing I saw were three cop cars; she was handcuffed and put in the backseat of a patrol car. That's what happens when one threatens to kill oneself.

I know she liked living here; she was friends with lots of people, enjoyed the cats, and liked watching DVDs from the lending library at the office. It was a safe place for her—albeit she couldn't have methy friends over, but she understood that rule, sort of.

She had asked if she could have friends over who weren't using, but I told her no. Sounds harsh, but I can't drug test every person creeping onto the property at all hours. And in her mind, if they weren't using at exactly that second, then they weren't using.

I couldn't continue with the tumult that her presence presented. I was tired of chasing cars through the park like some frantic, manic poodle running after cranked squirrels. People complained about trespassing meth heads and change stolen out of unlocked vehicles. It had to stop.

Sadie was hospitalized under a suicide watch.

Still no response from Sadie's mom or stepdad. I had the lawyer draw up the eviction notice and called Sadie's mom and asked if they would accept the notice as her legal guardians.

The mother didn't reply. The stepfather's message read: "Randy (sic) We are not Sadie's guardians. It's your responsibility to deliver the eviction notice to her. Don't contact us again unless it's through your attorney."

I got butthurt, then angry because I thought we agreed that this would be the last chance, and Sadie's mom ghosting me doesn't prevent what's going to happen.

Sadie's mom had mentioned before that Sadie almost broke up her marriage; but to allow a husband to control what was going on was cowardice. What a dick. He should be on that national registry of asshats.

I understand that having a child like Sadie would be difficult and tiresome. And that the child would never become a fully capable adult; thus, the parenting would never end. There would never be a cut-off date.

I'd attempted to protect this woman-child and smugly thought her mother appreciated it. Evidently not. You want me to spend dollars on attorneys' fees, why? It won't change the outcome. Was this to punish me for not allowing her to stay?

You thought for the price of rent that you'd have a full-time babysitter as well? Well, yeah you did, and I was one for quite a while.

Now the babysitter has resigned, and you're pissed off.

Sadie's therapist showed up at the park perhaps five days later. Nice woman. I walked her through the recent drama.

The therapist said that Sadie was still hospitalized under suicide watch because they couldn't stabilize her, that she hadn't been able to get a reply from Sadie's mom, and that Sadie's biggest worry was that she wouldn't have any place to live.

Sadie's mom didn't bother to call the therapist, but she did, while Sadie was under suicide watch, call Sadie and threaten to sell the RV and her belongings, which is like yelling "jump" at a guy on a ledge.

Upon learning that, it made me reevaluate my opinion of her mom. Did she want Sadie to do it? Why would you goad a clearly suicidal girl?

I told the therapist that since Sadie would be in lockdown for thirty days, she could still come back and be here for an additional thirty days under the eviction notice until she could locate another place to live. It was not as if I would evict her in absentia, and after learning how her mother was acting, I couldn't be another shitty adult.

I then asked the therapist, "Wouldn't the best thing for Sadie be a group home and some type of part-time volunteer work? She's lonely, has too much time on her hands, and that's when things turn ugly."

The therapist said we agreed on that, and she would try to organize a plan.

Unfortunately, that was not how things turned out.

Sadie was finally well enough to leave the hospital. Her mother gave her bus fare so she and a friend could go down to a city an hour away.

I learned this from the therapist.

This was not what I wanted for her, dammit. She wouldn't do well without some responsible adult supervision, and I have no idea who this "friend" was. It was none of my business, but I was very angry at her mother for simply bussing her out of town. I understood that Sadie was stressful, and she was tired of it, but still...This was just wrong.

A month passed, and I finally got a call from Sadie's mom. She was chirpy and pleasant, as if nothing troubling happened between us, as she said, "I guess Sadie is getting evicted, so we'll come move the trailer out." I told her the amount of back rent, and they paid it.

I was cordial, but aloof, finished with being nice to these asshats. I watched out for your child and put up with a lot of crap, and you took advantage of that. I don't like you. I did, but now I don't.

Sadie would have thrived in a group home with her loneliness at bay. With a part-time job or volunteering, she would have kept busy and away from the crackheads. She would have been fantastic at the animal shelter. Now? Who knows? I tried my best, and it wasn't good enough. None of this was my business, but dammit.

With Sadie gone, the constant procession of addicts ceased. I hoped Sadie was okay and safe.

TIME OUT

My bestie author friend said, "Fine. If you want to rail about asshats all the livelong day, you need to serve up an amuse bouche to cleanse the readers' palate for your next course of unrelenting catastrophe and apocalyptic distress." (Thus, the pleasant photos interspersed with the mayhem.)

Okay, so no asshats for a hot minute. Settle back, hydrate, gently stretch, and enjoy the following.

During the pandemic, a gentleman moved in for contract work in the area and was going to be on the property for six months or so.

He would leave on the weekends to visit family and friends. Very pleasant guy—late thirties, cute, just an all-around nice guy from what I saw. Steady job, running truck, was close with his family.

There was a woman who moved in shortly after; she was a divorcee from an utter bastard of an ex.

She was wonderful—friendly, sweet, and especially funny. She had a great sense of humor, even after an ugly divorce from an ugly man. She was a very attractive woman in her early forties with a winning smile, a full-time job, a good truck, and a great dog.

It just so happened that they ended up living in adjacent sites.

Then suddenly, he wasn't leaving on the weekends to visit friends and family anymore.

I didn't even consider romantic possibilities; I had two open sites that overlooked the neighbor's pasture of fat black and white cows and their babies in the spring, and in the summer, rows and rows of whispering corn.

Sounds dumb, but if I close my eyes, I can hear the drying harvest, the corn gravid, and the wind pushing through every layer of the field. That rustling, where weighty stalks make warm wind sing, was very soothing.

If you get a chance, stop on the side of a country road beside a corn field in high summer and listen.

It's special, no joke. And not in the creepy *Children of the Corn* way. That sound, the breeze on your skin, it's just magical.

It gives me shivers. It makes me feel small in a good way. Like when I'm dead all of this will continue. It's reassuring.

I'm Helen Keller when it comes to seeing attraction between people, so when I'd see them leaving in her or his truck, I'd just wave.

Then I'd see them pulling out kayaks in his or her truck and I'd also wave. No big deal, not my business. Enjoy your day.

After a while, this Helen realized they were a thing. Of course, with my misanthropic mindset, I couldn't hold out false hope... that new car smell doesn't last forever.

Eventually, nature's planned obsolescence would step in and destroy the relationship and the breakup would be awful.

Awkwardness would lie in the aftermath, echoing the trauma of an ugly high school breakup. You're broken up, but he's still sitting next to you IN SOCIAL STUDIES AND ENGLISH!

That would be horrible living side by side with dashed hopes and dreams, your ex too close... but wait, probably one or both would leave, and I'd need to fill those sites from the waiting list and who was next on that list?

Just super-fast thoughts in my noggin, looking for contingencies, but again, it's only concerning selfish me because there will be a possible site or two opening.

Okay, back to love...

DAMMIT, sorry, story interrupted because at nine o'clock tonight, right now, one of the T-Rexes had to *ding dong ding dong* and ask if a package arrived. Since all packages are on the counter behind him, um, no, whatever package you were waiting for would be right behind you. Turn around, T-Rex, turn around.

Goodnight and back to hopeful love.

He moved after his contract was completed, and she stayed on. Packages continued to be delivered to the campground for him, and she would pick them up. I realized that the relationship was continuing long distance and of course my ugly cynical brain snickered smugly that this wouldn't last.

But I seemed to be wrong.

Which pleased me.

She said he was coming up for kayaking and then other fun stuff, like maybe a hike. When she spoke of him, she was transcendent.

When I saw them leaving with the two kayaks, I waved.

Later, she told me with a brilliant grin that he was coming back for hunting season! They had a date for a hunting trip, and he would be up for the whole weekend!

I saw them that weekend and waved as they were leaving the park.

They waved back.

Hope you enjoyed your amuse bouche. Now back to campground fun and games.

CPS, IT'S ME AGAIN

A nice guy, mid-thirties, arrived to ask for a spot. He seemed pleasant and was vetted by two people at the park that knew him. He took an application and returned it for approval. I saw no problems with his background, so I agreed.

The site was for his ex-girlfriend and their three-year-old son. A spot had opened, and I let him know it was available now. It was August and a site opening was rare. He said they wanted to start in September. I said I wouldn't hold a spot that long. He then said they'd come in on August 9th.

He didn't arrive until the following day to drop off his three-year-old son, but the girlfriend showed up early with a two-man team of RV towers waiting to set up.

She reluctantly climbed out of her vehicle and looked around with a moue of distaste. Obviously, this dump was not up to her standards. She was a very pretty woman, kinda looked like Snow White, but bitterness hardened the set of her mouth.

Good lord, this is going to be fun.

I walked over, began to introduce myself, and she blurted, very upset, "I am here against my will. I don't want to be here. I hate this place."

Well, that outburst was unexpected since most people who are here are happy to be so. This was the first kidnap victim to be installed on the property.

Okay, we can solve this. I said, "Alright, come to the office. I'll refund you, and you can go elsewhere."

"No. No, I don't have anywhere else to go."

OMG you entitled little shit. I ignored her and helped the two dudes set up because she wasn't doing anything but bitching about her predicament and the ugliness of her surroundings.

I then got her paperwork from the office, went back to the RV, and handed it to her. There was no thank you, and no apology for her rude behavior. She simply took the papers and shut the door in my face. Okay.

The day after she moved in, he'd brought their child to her. I watched him hand his beloved son to her; she treated the boy like a bag of dog food. She hefted him up without hugging, smiling, or talking to him and deposited him in the RV, turned back to her ex and continued whatever argument she'd been saving up.

I was told by several tenants that she spent a lot of time banging around in her RV. This happened on her first night, then the second. That wasn't a fortuitous harbinger of things to come...

Well, she did tell me she didn't want to be here. I can make that happen and nip this in the bud.

Three days after she moved in, she attempted to return the signed rental contract and I shook my head. "Nope, you are not staying here. This is not going to work out; it's a very bad fit. I emailed your boyfriend, and he will move you out. You can stay until September 1st."

"But what if I want to stay?" She pouted.

Are you freaking kidding me? You don't want to be here, you said that to my face, and now that I say you can leave, you want to stay?

I calmly replied, "I have a waiting list of people who really want to be here, and again, this is not a good fit. You already told me you didn't want to be here."

She argued, "You don't understand! I just broke up with my boyfriend of 12 years!"

I really wanted to respond with, "Hey Pouty, people break up all the time, get over it, get a job, move on. You're 45 plus years old with a small child. Cool your jets on the selfishness. At least he moved you to a quiet RV park with families and a playground for your child. And he paid your rent."

But I didn't say a thing, it was not my business. She thought the world had treated her unfairly, and she deserved so much more. One cannot argue with such a strongly held opinion.

Self-pity should be the eighth deadly sin.

Back to Pouty…

"I don't really care about that. It's been decided, you will move out September first."

Pouty: "But I haven't bothered anyone."

She had already begun to annoy the neighbors—one woman across the road said she came over and started handing her random stuff. Another woman said she spent a good amount of time the night before stomping and talking loudly in her RV. I thought about her little boy and my stomach sank.

I repeated, "You are not staying here."

She dropped the papers on the counter outside the office and stalked away. I called the ex- boyfriend and told him what occurred. He'd earlier replied to my email and said he'd arrange to move her out. I assumed she also called the ex-boyfriend and pitched a fit.

The ex-boyfriend arrived, quickly packed up her and the baby, and his sister drove to the campground and took them down to her house to stay. He hooked up the RV to his truck to take it off the property, and I refunded his money. I was grateful that his young son would be living with his aunt, glad there would be another adult presence in that household.

The ex-boyfriend wasn't annoyed that he had to get her out of the park; it was as if he knew it wouldn't work out. Maybe he knew it wouldn't work out anywhere if he wasn't with her.

I did tell the ex-boyfriend it was none of my business, and then pushed myself into his business and told him he'd better get custody of his little three-year-old.

In the short time she was here, I never saw her interact positively with the child. Out in the yard, she ignored him. Acting like that in public worried me about what happened when he was inside the RV. I thought about her stomping and talking loudly enough to alarm the neighbors. How scary must it have been for the toddler *inside* the RV with his mother.

If she had stayed, I would have called CPS. She had such a fundamental lack of caring that frightened me. Her tiny boy was alone with her anger and discontent, and that chilled me.

I dreaded to think what that woman would do to that little boy when she realized her ex had moved on to a new partner. He told me he was dating someone. I don't think she knew, and I certainly wasn't going to tell her.

That little boy looked just like his father. Was he a constant reminder of a failed relationship? A symbol of her disappointment? Is that why she treated her son so coldly?

I thought if she got a new man, she wouldn't give a shit and would grant the father full custody.

She was very pretty, so one can only hope that another brave but daring guy came along and accepted that perilous mission.

YOU ARE THE WORST

Ben, his girlfriend, and his pit bull moved in; he did have a job at the time and claimed he was a "carpenter."

I didn't know about the pit bull until after the fact, and then it was too late… remember, pandemic?

He was chronically unemployed and took no blame for his inability to hold a job. His girlfriend was on disability, and the pit bull was supposedly her service dog.

I found that hard to believe, not that he was chronically unemployed, but that the pit bull was a service dog. The "service animal" paperwork he printed off the internet had as much value as my Universal Life Church reverend certificate.

I allowed it because there may have been a slight infinitesimal chance that it was a service dog, but generally the only breed we do not accept are pit bulls. Bulldogs of course, but not the pit bull. My camp host and I have been bitten by that breed.

They were quiet tenants. I only had to go a couple times to shut down the domestic disputes that had ratcheted up enough to alarm the neighbors. Again, stop fighting in a metal box, we all can hear you.

Maybe my notion of "quiet" has gotten skewed.

All y'all have watched *COPS* right? There's that shirtless, sinewy guy who has super ratty tattoos, with greasy Jesus hair, and you know he smells. If a louse crawled across his forehead to get away from that funk, it wouldn't be a surprise.

Ben's girlfriend's father Luke also lived on the property in a separate RV. He was an older model of Ben with less hair and more rancor.

Luke, the father, was creepy in a wash your window with a moist filthy rag during a red light while hungrily staring at your legs kinda way. *Ugh.*

When I mowed behind his RV, there were plastic bins filled with empty liquor bottles and mounds of cigarette butts in the fire pit. The number of discards alone were more suitable for a large rave but were simply his weekend's accumulation.

I never interacted with Ben's girlfriend. She stayed in the RV with her "service dog." It had several litters of puppies, which they sold. I warned them one more litter and I'm calling animal control for abuse. No service dog should be distracted by having puppies, and it's twisted that that poor dog is how you're making rent. That isn't a service dog, it's a one bitch puppy mill. Get a job.

The pandemic hit, and they hit the jackpot. Ben, of course, immediately blamed the pandemic for why he couldn't hold a job and said they wouldn't be paying rent for the foreseeable future. The eviction moratorium provided that if the landlord was notified in writing that a tenant wouldn't be paying rent, they could not be evicted for nonpayment. Okay, but they both are getting stimulus checks which a portion should be going to rent, and the girlfriend is on disability. Stop blaming the pandemic for your lazy ass. Days after the second round of stimulus checks, he drove onto the campground with a new car. So, he now had two cars, his girlfriend didn't drive, still no job, and the rent was months behind.

That frosted me. I couldn't evict him for not paying rent. I couldn't evict him for the faux service dog. That pandemic moratorium was killing me.

I thought about it and realized that his new car was not agreed to on the rental contract and approval was required for each vehicle. God, I love a well-crafted rental agreement!

I could evict his brand-new vehicle. That was a capital idea!

I sent him a notice stating that the new vehicle was not authorized and would be towed. He needed to move it off the property immediately. If he didn't remove it, I would.

Ben was enraged. How dare I! This is from the guy who planned to milk this pandemic for every extension of the moratorium. It's funny in hindsight, his outrage, that is. It's like he couldn't see his own bad behavior whatsoever. He was the victim here.

To retrieve Ben's car after towing, it would cost tow fees and storage. And if it came back here, away it would go again! We can do this all day if you want! Dude, there goes the rest of your stimulus check!

I know it was petty, childish revenge on an opportunistic, conniving asshat, but it felt good. I was not above sinking to his level.

As per the state's towing laws, the car had a three-day towing notice posted on the windshield. He must have really loved that new car because he moved out within two days of that notice.

I later learned he was the "caretaker" at another RV park in town. I felt bad for those people because Ben always looked for the angle with which to take advantage. He was the guy who offered to help the drunk girl at the party. Yeah, no.

I never let him "work" for me because he was that guy who planned on "spraining" an ankle while mowing. He always looked for the grift. He would effortlessly walk into Rite Aid to buy crutches while on the phone with his contingency fee lawyer to sue for permanent and lifelong damages.

Father's Day rolled around, and the girlfriend showed up at the park with the pit bull to be dropped off by Ben—both of whom were banned from the campground for nonpayment of rent and general assholery.

There was no reason she had to be on the property. Ben and his girlfriend wanted to rub themselves in my face in an insulting way, like hahaha we can do what we want.

They knew and disregarded the ban. Luke, the father, was furious when I told her to leave the park or get cited for trespass.

Luke argued he wanted his daughter to visit on Father's Day. I retorted, "Then go to her RV and visit with her. She's not welcome here, and you know why. She's a deadbeat and so is her boyfriend."

I told him to stop quarreling with me and meet up with her off property.

I thought he was going to hit me when Ben and the girlfriend drove off the property—that poor pit bull in the back seat most likely pregnant again—and he cursed me vehemently and wished for my death.

I said, "Go over to their house." Luke said he wasn't talking to Ben; they got in a fight. I said, "I don't care."

He cursed and cursed that I ruined his Father's Day. He could have prevented all this drama by simply meeting her at a cafe for lunch. Or driven over and visited her at her RV. Or they could have gone to a park and had a picnic. The beach is ten minutes away. There were countless options, but he wanted the one that wasn't available.

Luke wanted the one which offered the least effort on his part.

After a couple of minutes of being harangued by Luke, I'd had enough. I felt myself entering mean girl range, and I wanted to say:

"For you, Father's Day is a joke. You can't make up for all the years you were a crackhead, and she'll never forgive you so it's too late to make amends. You never got her orthodontics so that's why she won't smile, and all your drug use left you with six rotten teeth which just screams your bad habits. She's ashamed of you and what you represent. You never went to her back-to-school nights, or paid child support so stop pretending this one inconvenient moment ruined your relationship with your daughter. You've already accomplished that all by yourself. Don't you see who she chose for a mate? It's a copy of you and he's a worthless, unemployed, weaselly asshole with no promise of a future. Ben is the obvious result of what a shit parent you are. People either marry their mother or father, and I really doubt her mother is that big of a cunt."

But I didn't because he was beyond livid and hadn't stopped his diatribe of murder and sexual insults and that retort most likely would earn me a punch in the face. He was so wound-up spittle bubbles collected in the corners of his mouth. Other tenants stepped outside to watch, phones in hand.

Pick your battles. Consider your co-pay.

Okay, maybe this was the bad guy Bunny was talking about? (You haven't gotten to that part yet, sorry.)

Enough. I held up my hand and said calmly, "You are out of line, and you will be evicted." Even though the moratorium was in place, I needed to say something to make this stop.

He sputtered, "I'm leaving. I'm not living here." And proceeded to cuss me out with a magnificent hatred and limited vocabulary.

I walked away, a little shaky in the knees. He did move out shortly, and for that I was grateful. He left all of his garbage, which I removed with heavy duty gloves and numerous trash bags.

He also left a couple of rancidly malevolent voice messages, which I was like, *dude, if something happens to me, these will be played in court.*

You better hope nobody else murders me in the meantime.

P.S. Talk about a weird coincidence... one of the guys here bought Luke's old motorhome and while renovating it, he called the sheriffs to come out and confiscate all the drug paraphernalia, empty vials, and syringes he found jammed behind the paneling in the dining area. Yeah, not a big surprise.

TOO MANY TEENAGERS

The family moved in a couple months before the pandemic began—a mother and three teenaged daughters, and a fourth older daughter who allegedly would only be visiting occasionally and only during the day with her father, the mother's ex-husband.

The RV was 18' in length.

The eldest daughter's boyfriend wanted to move in, and without my knowledge, had already been there for a few weeks on the down low. I had approved him and then learned that news from a neighbor.

I told the mother that the father and other daughter were not allowed to stay, but they continued to sneak onto the property late at night. Now there were at least six people in that tiny trailer. Let's not forget the two chihuahuas. Well, their barking won't let you forget them.

They were messy and cluttered. There were too many people with too much stuff. Numerous plastic storage bins were jammed under the RV since the RV itself was already jammed with people.

There have been studies showing that the more crowded rats get, the more aggressive they become. Just saying… Before long, there was so much drama going on in that small space. On more than one occasion, I knocked on their door and yelled over the nonstop shrill barking to shut those dogs up. They were home but did nothing to stop them. I don't know how they could stand it.

I hall monitored and turned all their teenaged friends away. The mom was at work, and there were too many teenagers showing up. **DURING THE PANDEMIC!!!!!!**

This was tiring and scary. They wore their masks chin length or below the nose, if at all. I told them their friends cannot use the restrooms, but then on my cameras they are all going in there like it was prom night. I was already cleaning the restrooms twice a day, trying to keep the invisible Covid threat at bay. I didn't need the extra exposure to strangers' germs and increased cleaning duties. Remember the run on toilet paper? The jacked-up prices? I do.

There was a constant odor of weed and vape wafting from their RV. This was turning into a flop house. I got the feeling the mother was trying to be her daughters' best friend. Out of all the people living there, there seemed to be no responsible adult. *Ugh.*

The cherry on this drama pie was the daughter's boyfriend was physically abusive. Disputes ensued and the cops were called and called again. Why are fists even a choice? And why is the mother allowing this boyfriend to stay?

This would not end well.

One of the daughters may be on the spectrum, no big deal, but the issue was that no one was monitoring her behavior or believing she could do any wrong.

This daughter ended up on my porch, my private residence. While my front door was ajar, she came in and looked around from the entry area and I told her to get out right now. There was clear signage outside stating don't enter, private residence, and yet, there she was... and this did not happen just once.

When this was relayed to her mother, the mother denied it and said that her other daughter watched her very closely and that this did not occur.

When the mother was told that her daughter most likely let the goats out and was chasing them through the park, the mother denied it, stating that could never ever possibly happen.

After this family moved in, someone had started to peel the paint from the women's bathroom stalls. The mother denied, denied,

denied it, but why was that kid in the bathroom for hours on end? A bathroom during a pandemic was not the best hangout at the park.

When the mother was told there were photos showing her daughter lying in the middle of the road—where enormous, shiny milk trucks did their morning runs to the dairies, she denied it outright, went ballistic and shrieked that I was harassing her.

She refused to look at the photos and denied her daughter would ever do such a thing.

Here I was trying to keep her daughter safe, and she just could not acknowledge there may be a problem.

Deny, deny, deny. I wasn't criticizing her child, but she took everything I said personally. It wasn't about her, but she took it that way.

It all came to a head in December 2020, during a wild nighttime hailstorm. She and her oldest daughter rang the bell, and I came down to the office. She partially paid the past due rent. I asked them to stay out of the office and I would bring the receipt out. I was wearing a mask, she was not. The daughter's mask was below her chin.

I handed her the receipt and said over the pinging of the hail hitting the metal roof that she should begin to look for a new place to live (at this point, the moratorium would be lifted in January 2021.) I wanted to give her a heads up; it would be a good idea to find another place before the moratorium expired because there would be a **lot** of people moving at that time. I had my eviction list lined up and knew several park managers were doing the same.

The rage that erupted from the mother was stunning.

All I said was, "Your being here is not a good fit; you should begin to look for another place to live."

It swiftly degenerated into her daughter holding her back as the mother swung at me, arms flailing, fists inches from my face as I leaned backward, got my balance, then backed up. This moment scared me. I was three weeks away from two scheduled spinal surgeries, so I wasn't moving like my usual ninja self.

This uncontrollable fury didn't make sense. They'd been repeatedly warned of their behavior. The only reason they hadn't been evicted was because of the moratorium, so the mother, couldn't in a rational world, believe the shenanigans going on in their site were reasonable and not alarming. And why would she think punching me would improve the situation?

While I and their immediate neighbors patiently suffered these asshats, of course the moratorium was then extended until July of 2021. Their antics continued; they didn't move out. If there was any change in behavior, they got worse.

The smell of weed was overwhelming; it gushed from the interior of the RV and floated out the open windows, past the incessant, nails on chalkboard yapping of those neglected little dogs. They were running a dopey day care for all the truants in the neighborhood.

I worked very hard at keeping their friends out. Can you imagine the blowback if a minor overdosed on the property from whatever else they were using? It wouldn't be my fault but that wouldn't stop the lawsuits.

I was getting copyright infringement notices for internet piracy; games and movies were being illegally downloaded. I assumed they were the culprits because there were four plus teenagers and all their friends. Why not steal movies and get high? I printed out the copyright infringement notices and passed them out to all tenants, but I specifically asked the teenagers and young adults (14-19) if they were downloading SIMS and a bunch of other games.

Imagine their mock outrage and stunned insulted looks, followed with snarky anger and denials. Did I accuse everyone else in the park? Or just them? I hate that *but what about them?* We aren't talking about *them*; we are talking about *you*.

Sorry, but they were the online thieves by a process of elimination; it was not the 75-year-old dude in the park pirating *SIMS, Call of Duty* and *Grand Theft Auto* or the 86-year-old grandma who didn't know how to log onto Hulu without my help, or the aged gentlemen who worked a full-time job at Goodwill and borrowed DVDs from the lending library since he didn't know how to stream.

This continued for weeks, and I was still getting these notices because as the owner of the WIFI, I was responsible for these downloads and the accompanying penalties. They didn't give a shit.

Let me digress for a minute. If my landlord hinted I should move, I'd move. I'm not psychic but that suggestion carries a lot of prophecy for the future.

They never considered changing their behavior or looking for a new place. Their denial was alarming; it was as if the future would never get here.

Imagine their consternation when finally, the moratorium was lifted, and they were served. Oh my, this was a complete surprise, and they were stunned!

So that meant no rent was paid, all their trash piled up, and dog poop was everywhere. These were such childish acts of revenge.

The strange thing was the mother was at least fifty years old. Did she think this nasty behavior wouldn't have consequences? How do you teach your children cause and effect if you don't believe in it yourself?

The day they exited the property, owing rent, with arms raised out of the open Suburban's windows to flip me off all the way to the main highway while screaming obscenities, I thought, *good riddance, things will quiet down,* and they did.

The piracy notices stopped. Surprise!

I removed up their trash and abandoned refrigerator and had the water spigot replaced because they pulled off faucet's top for shits and giggles.

A couple of weeks later, a well-groomed guy stopped by in a very shiny black BMW. He had on a shiny gold watch and was wearing fashionable, clean clothes. And there I was in muck-covered Wellingtons, torn jeans, a misshapen stained sweater, and a ponytail decorated with random flecks of hay. We hailed from different planets. Oh, and he smelled wonderful.

He introduced himself as a property manager based in Portland but had properties in this county. He asked about the too many teenagers and mother and said he had one open site at his park and wanted my opinion.

I told him about their chaotic lifestyle, and the girl who nobody watched. I then told him they didn't pay the final rent, and I had to clean their site filled with broken glass, cigarette butts, and just general filth. I told him that the mom tried to punch me and was only thwarted because the daughter held her back. That there were remarkable lapses in judgment and anger management in that flock of folks.

He said they told him everyone in the park was evicted.

I looked at him, up the road at all the rear ends of RVs and shrugged. I didn't understand why they would say everyone was evicted, oh, wait, oh, that was funny.

I explained they each got letters of eviction and by law one includes an eviction notice to All Other Occupants.

All Other Occupants in your RV site, dumbass. I don't know the accurate inventory of how many sketchy teenage trolls you got tucked away in there.

He laughed about that and thanked me for my time. Everything I said to him was the truth, so it was up to him to figure out if he wanted them as tenants.

About a month later, a couple tenants said the mother's teenagers' bike were left behind and had been chained to their RV. Go figure. They asked if they could cut the chain and dump the bikes in the trash.

"Absolutely," I said. Especially after they mentioned emailing, texting, and calling them with no response.

They also told me that the too many teenagers family was running around town bad mouthing me about kicking them out and that they couldn't find another place to live, and it was all my fault. My fault? Christ, why didn't they think about that before they became a nuisance?

I would have given a neutral reference if they had just vamoosed when I asked.

Just a couple of reminders if you want to live in a decent, reasonably priced, quiet, and calm environment:

- Don't take a swing at me when I tell you staying here is not a good fit—kinda begs the question.
- Don't let your daughter vandalize the bathroom stalls.
- Don't let your flock of chihuahuas poop everywhere and not pick it up, especially on the sidewalk in front of the women's restroom.
- Don't have the cops come every two weeks because nobody in your household has any sort of anger management.
- Tell your teenage daughters to stop calling 911 and threaten to kill themselves.
- Stop breaking your own shit! Everyone can hear you!
- Stop inviting numerous teenage friends to crash every day. This is not a flop house.
- Stop allowing everyone you know to use the ladies' restroom, only tenants are allowed.
- Don't let your daughter lie down in the middle of the street taking selfies where the dairy trucks do their daily runs.
- Don't pirate video games and movies.
- Don't allow your daughter to sit in front of the office for hours on end playing music as loud as possible.
- If the sign outside the private residence says, "private property," tell your daughter to get out of my house.
- Don't cuss out the camp host.
- Don't let your daughter free the goats to run through the campground.
- And finally… pay rent.

P.S. None of the above rules should even have to be listed.

NASTY WIFE, NASTY LIFE

A woman and her husband assumed that since they rented the site, they could do as they pleased. I've seen that attitude before and, sir and good lady, not likely.

This short guy just seemed to always overdo the macho guy thing.

When I had to deal with Shorty, I felt like I was Thor looming over him, and he blustered ever more aggressively because of that.

Think of a little bantam rooster annoyingly pecking at your ankles. You want to give it a swift kick, but you don't, because a part of you feels sorry for the little stupid cretin. He just cannot help himself; it is his nature.

The wife was very displeased with the world. All of it. To say she was not a smiler would be an understatement. I'd bet she even hated cheese enchiladas and sunsets. Her face was perpetually pinched, and her wrinkles formed into those grooves.

Her dissatisfaction was clearly etched on her face.

I stopped waving hello and goodbye long before this incident. I don't need my mellow harshed by her ugly aura.

In the past, there was a laundry on the property. Unfortunately, over time, the levels of phosphorus and other chemicals were harming the biological makeup of the wastewater treatment plant.

These biological issues were compounded by the discharge of laundry water into the wastewater treatment system which diluted the influent and caused issues with meeting plant permits for BOD and TSS. Okay, I'll stop.

I closed the laundry. People were pissed. Guys, there are three laundries in town. Just don't get banned like QAnon mom and you'll do fine. (She's in the subsequent book, part Deux.)

Imagine my surprise when a washing machine was delivered to their site. This was after the notice to all that the laundry was closed because of blah, blah, blah.

I traipsed up there and told them this was not allowed. I relayed this over the nonstop barking of three dogs outside their door behind a much too flimsy metal fence. I thought they only had two dogs. Where did that aggressive third one come from? That fence is not going to hold.

Of course, she replied that she can do what she wanted on her land. And, she added with barely repressed venom, that memo I sent out about alternating sites, odd, even, for black and gray discharge (that's to even out the flow to the waste treatment plant so I'm not deluged with 50 sites discharging all at once) she said she was not going to do that. She will do what she wants on her land, she repeated.

What was with this "my land" syndrome? Girl, I'm the owner here, and even *I* don't really own it. I'm just enjoying it for a time and caretaking it for the next person who comes along. Remember, you can't take it with you.

Again, this happened during the pandemic, and it was not enough of a reason to evict, said the attorney. Great, great, but wait… I reviewed their rental agreement, and there were only *two* shitty dogs on their lease, not three.

Okay, just like Ben when I evicted his new car, I'm gonna evict that extra dog… and that was exactly what I did. All pets needed prior approval per the rental agreement and once again, thank God for a well-crafted contract.

By the way, these dogs were not cared for or trained. The neighbor to their north had already told me next time their vicious dogs got loose, he was going to shoot them because they immediately ran over and tore at his timid female lab who was tethered outside.

I prepared a notice that the third dog on their "property" was not agreed to and must be removed.

I printed it, folded it into an envelope, and stood outside their unit for a good ten minutes. Those dogs went mad less than two feet away in their fenced area as I knocked, knocked, knocked. The metal fence bowed as the dogs barreled into it; I flipped my pepper spray open, just in case one cleared the fence.

I must remind them for the nth time that they needed to pick up their dogs' poop; there was a large rusty metal bucket of watery shit right next to their front door. That's not really considered cleaning up after one's dogs. In fact, if there's any breeze, that noxious odor from that overfull bucket would waft right inside their open windows.

Imagine living next to three large dogs that barked nonstop outside your bedroom window, just ten feet away, when you worked the night shift at the cheese factory. I looked over to Cheryl's windows with the shades drawn and winced; I knew this was screwing with her sleep.

They took nuisance to a new level. It got old walking up there to bang on the side of their RV, dodging the jumping dogs trying to take a piece out of my arm, to tell them to bring them inside and shut them up.

I wouldn't leave until they answered the door. I'd wait.

Finally, the door opened an inch and I held out the notice and slipped it through the opening. She grabbed it and slammed the door, which closed with a soft, plastic click. I'm sure it wasn't satisfying.

After the dog notice, she emailed and said I was no longer allowed on her property to drop off any notices, and no, she would not give me her mailing address. She said she never wanted to hear from me again. She refused to acknowledge the landlord- tenant relationship based on a signed, legal contract. It made me smile.

Her sense of entitlement was awe inspiring. Who put her in charge? If you are in charge, boss, you're welcome to clean the men's and women's restrooms. Now that's an adventure in entrepreneurship. Things you can't unsee.

My notice to her stated that the new dog was not on the original application and must be removed or it would be removed by animal control. I gave her a specific date that this would occur.

They must have loved that awful dog because they made the decision to leave.

No, they didn't love that dog, but their son did, who I found out had been sneaking onto the property and living there after his girlfriend kicked him out. That dog was his.

Another notice went out to them, the son must apply to live here and it would be an extra $120.00 a month for another adult in their RV.

Nasty woman emailed me and said they wouldn't pay. I emailed back and said then the son (in his mid-thirties) was banned from the property and would be trespassed by the authorities and that the son's dog was still going to be removed by animal control.

We had this stalemate for a week or so, and then they moved out, without paying the rent due, of course.

Their final gracious gesture was to take their large pail of dog shit they rarely emptied and dumped it all over the site.

What was it with these scatological displays?

The irony was that I spent several hours a day in a wastewater treatment facility on the property dealing with shit, so frankly, a little more doesn't faze me.

I cleaned up the site, emptied the fire pit of cigarette butts, and shoveled up the dog shit soup. I then added flowers and grass seed to the dog mauled lawn and had it rented in a couple days.

A couple weeks later, I had a surprise visit from the DEQ (Department of Environmental Quality, a state agency in charge of just about everything in nature).

Nasty woman and Shorty had reported me for toxic discharges on the premises, and he needed to inspect the site. The caller's identity was supposed to be confidential, but I gave the guy their names and he nodded agreeably.

Backstory, Shorty with the short guy mentality absolutely loathed the 6-foot 5-inch lumberjack living next door and complained constantly that the lumberjack's truck dripped motor oil into his site.

Several times I came out to their "property" to investigate and found that no, there was no evidence of leakage. I'm talking no more than a half cup under the truck, which could have also been condensation dripping from the undercarriage or the result of puddles from the rain.

Shorty's strident belief that this massive Exxon Valdez was polluting his site compelled him to start digging a trench to move the "oil" away from his area.

Shorty was literally digging up the road beneath the logger's truck for an imaginary leak. This was a delusion driven by height envy and morphed into rage. Talk about taking "touching my stuff" to new heights…

I went over and told Shorty to fill in that trench or he'd be evicted for vandalism. He gave me a look, and I added calmly that I would file a police report for criminal mischief as well. His choice. He glared up at me. I didn't care.

He filled in the trench, but held that grudge, fed it, and read it stories at bedtime. It held him tightly, sitting on his shoulders even after he exited the property and compelled him to call the DEQ on the guy that had a good fourteen inches on him in height and no leaking truck. He also did it in the hopes that I'd get in trouble.

The DEQ guy inspected the area and I explained that this was merely a revenge call. There were no fines or penalties since there wasn't an unlawful discharge.

More time passed and I forgot about them and their antics. I got a call from a woman at a storage facility north of me who said that she had this number as the nasty lady and short guy's residential address. I explained that they had moved out, and she told me a story that had her at her wits' end:

Nasty lady and Shorty rented a storage site from her, but their junk overflowed the assigned area. Their trucks and equipment were leaking oil and fluids all over the ground. Isn't that ironic?

They also stopped paying rent and were being asshats and telling her they could do what they wanted. Geez, it was the only song they know.

Oh, wait, I had an idea!

I recommended that she write to them the following missive. Dear Nasty Lady and Shorty: You have been warned on numerous occasions that your vehicles and equipment are actively leaking hazardous materials into the ground. Even after numerous notices, you have taken no action to remediate the pollution. You must vacate the property within ten days and pay rent due in full. If you ignore this final notice, the DEQ will be contacted and provided photographs of your discharge of toxic chemicals. For your information, the DEQ daily penalties for deliberate discharge of hazardous wastes run in the hundreds if not thousands of dollars.

She called later and let me know that it did the trick. They paid the rent due, gathered all their junk, and moved to annoy a new crop of unsuspecting citizens.

You're welcome, my pleasure. Wouldn't have thought of it unless it had recently happened to me. Talk about karma.

Just a thought—wouldn't it be nice if there was a national registry of asshats?

MEAN DRUNKS

The Fellas

The fellas drink, drink, get mean drunk, pick on each other, pick on others, and fall into the blackberry brambles while trying to walk the neighbor's dog (without permission). No dog was harmed in this drunken adventure, but boy were the fellas scratched and bleeding. I'm sure they regretted that dog walk once they sobered up.

Of course, thankfully for them, they could never remember the day/night before, so when I recapped the prior night's litany of bad behavior, all I got back were puzzled looks.

There was a very lovely girl who was faced with one of the fellas' unwarranted, razor-sharp wrath when she asked them to turn down Predator (she lived five RVs down and knew where they were in the movie).

She related to me, "He said, 'Why don't you just git back on your Rascal and roll home to finish your dinners?'." (No Rascal was involved in this altercation, but you know how we women hate to be called fat.)

It really upset her because the fellas had a way of finding a soft spot and grinding their heels into it.

I approached the fellas' motorhome and kept a straight face (that Rascal comment was absurdly funny and very mean) and banged on the door for a good ten minutes. They routinely stayed up late, and it was 11:00 a.m.

Finally, the door creaked open, and I bitched at them. One of the fellas, dressed in a beautiful robe, said, "I don't remember any of that." So, of course I bark, "Don't let it happen again." Learning curve = flat.

Mean drunks. They are the worst. And they are drunk or high all the time. If your neighbor from five sites down knocks on your door and tells you she can hear your movie, it's *Predator*, please turn it down. Just turn it down, m'kay?

If your neighbors, two sites downwind of you, have COPD and asthma, don't leave your gigantic motorhome idling black exhaust for hours because you forgot to turn it off or got distracted by your jet engine loud DVD of *Predator*.

Why can't we just get along? And why are they always watching *Predator*?

You know what gets you kicked out? When you make me pay attention to your behavior, or you make me work harder. If I must listen to how your activities offended or alarmed others, that's when our relationship is going to end. Badly. My favorite tenants are the ones I forget live here, or who are simply pleasant and quiet, very quiet.

Tenants who complained water puddled outside their steps when the day before it rained two inches are the ones that got on my nerves and my short list.

I gave the mean drunks an eviction notice once the moratorium lifted and surprisingly, they got out without complaint. I didn't receive any calls regarding references, so lord knows where they went.

Just to be clear, this wasn't the first issue with them. There had been ongoing and serious complaints for quite a while. Their rental file was quite thick with warnings and finally we all had had enough.

I got a call from them in September 2021; they had moved out in July. I didn't pick up. I imagine the fellas had forgotten how they'd behaved. I hadn't.

ODOT Idiot

ODOT Idiot, and his equally drunk girlfriend moved onto the property. I didn't know they were serious drunks until they got here, although there was a clear clue. When they came in for an application, he had a beer between his legs…and he was driving.

ODOT is Oregon Department of Transportation. From my experiences with this singular state governmental employee, I commend ODOT for recruiting and training only the best and brightest! Not. This clown's job at ODOT was flagger. He's that guy with the STOP/SLOW sign when there's highway work going on.

ODOT Idiot's job, the flag pole's job, was to hold him upright and to sway enough to spin the sign from "Stop" to "Slow." Demanding work, highly stressful, much like an air traffic controller.

He got a paycheck while that poor penniless flagpole had to wait for him every day to wrap his sweaty, unwashed hand around it. It had to endure all that beer vapor from the night before and random sulfur farts all day that just reeked of malnutrition. I felt sorry for that flagpole.

His girlfriend didn't work and got social security disability. Things went quickly from bad to badder.

Lots of drinking, each of them, and arguments ensued. Maybe it was because most RVs are 300 square feet that condensed resentment and general angst brought out the worst in people—especially when excessive drinking culminated in vino veritas or vodka verdad. We have WIFI and DVDs, please just stream or play, stop picking fights with each other, or just take a nap and sleep it off.

Cops were called, but he didn't get arrested. Either he would veer off property and get on the highway to drunkenly threaten the public's health, or she would cancel the call. If they were both in the RV when the cops arrived, they simply would not answer the door.

There was a traveling nurse who worked nights at the local hospital stuck next to them. He asked me to move him. I apologized and promised I'd take care of the situation.

Back to fun and games with ODOT Idiot.

She would show up in the mornings with a black eye. I've never been punched in the eye, but it looked horrifically painful. Her brow, eyelids, under eye area, cheekbone, and side of her nose would be a swollen patchwork of yellow, purple, blue, while the whites of that abused eye were scarlet, congested with broken capillaries. Her eye looked like it hurt to blink. Her eye begged me to get her to a women's shelter. Just her eye because her mouth wouldn't say it. Ever.

Looking at her face made my face hurt.

She never applied coverage makeup, slipped on overlarge sunglasses or feebly blamed an errant door. She wore those bruises nonchalantly, and never once defended her injuries or commented on them. Those awful marks were just… there for the world to see. How did such degradation become commonplace?

He would drunkenly speed through the campground at all hours, and at that time besides the chickens running free and the numerous cats, there were a dozen children at the park that were home schooled because of the pandemic.

He would be so loaded that he couldn't drive in a straight line. He'd weave down the road, barely missing all the above.

That did it for me. Had he stayed in his RV and drunkenly assaulted his girlfriend, I imagine he would have stayed for an indeterminate period, until his girlfriend would wise up, tire of the constant beatdowns, file charges, get him arrested, have him plead out, and put him away.

Remember, Pandemic, moratorium. Let the hijinks ensue!

Once you put others at risk because of your disgusting behavior, you get a 24-hour notice of eviction. That was an expensive proposition, but it got the attorney ball rolling and got him served (not her because she was usually a passenger but evicting him would evict her as well. What? She's going to stay at the site without a RV? Or his loving embrace?

Legal eviction proceedings take longer than one would imagine. There's the filing, then service, then hearing, then either trial or an agreement, if there's a trial that takes a long time, there are witnesses and documents. But if there's an agreement, as in you'll get out in thirty days and we can drop this, based on how much the tenants know they can abuse the system, that can take even LONGER!

When my attorney and I were at the first hearing, both ODOT Idiot and his girlfriend showed up at the court and the bailiff said that without masks, they couldn't enter the courtroom.

Thus, these two knuckleheads, who snickered and whispered loud threats (in the courthouse corridor outside the courtroom) couldn't come in. The judge gave us a minute to see if we could resolve this.

I asked my attorney to get them out of the campground as fast as possible because they were a danger to others. He spoke with them and negotiated a mutually signed settlement that they would be out in thirty days, no later. They agreed to pay rent past and currently due.

Thirty days came and went, and please remember I'm getting them off the property as a danger to others, and they retaliated by continuing to drink heavily and be a bigger danger to others.

I continued to reassure the good people at the park that I was doing my best to get them evicted.

Now, they were violating the agreement we had made. The date of moveout came and went. They were still in the site and no rent was paid. We went back to court for the violation of settlement, and that additional order got served on them. They still did not move, and the nightly entertainment continued—they both thought it was hilarious to deliberately weave around the park's roads and scare people.

Kids stayed off the roads and stopped riding their bikes. ODOT Idiot didn't care how many people yelled at him; it didn't wipe that wasted grin off his face or slow him down behind the wheel.

The cops said they couldn't do anything on private property; it wasn't considered drunk driving or public intoxication because it wasn't city or county owned property.

My normal tenants rightfully complained, and I told them I'm doing the best I can. Laws are made to protect citizens, but then you have these horrendous asshats who relish inflicting fear and dragging out the misery of their presence, what else can I do but follow the law?

I went back to court to get the order of eviction. The sheriff served that, now they had an additional seven days on top of the days past the thirty days while this whole process was taking place. Oh, that day they should be out? Nope, still there. Now back to court for another order and the sheriff was alerted that they needed to be physically moved out. That took about another week to organize, and the morning the cops came to remove them, they were gone. They left like fifteen minutes before.

I had a feeling that they'd done this before, because the timing of their departure was impeccable.

They had been at the park for no more than three months when all this madness began and ended. Three months, most of which was spent in court or having documents served trying to remove them before they killed someone.

But for them, three month's free rent in a nice, quiet park that they could terrorize? What a deal!

I understand tenants' rights are very important, but it's frustrating when I'm trying to keep my tenants safe from awful people and I'm stymied by the tenants' protection laws.

One of these days, I must learn how to identify assholery from the get-go and save myself from attorney's fees and massive chaos.

Enough of ODOT Idiot, I'm sure he's been fired because the flagpole complained to HR about him not pulling his weight.

Again, can we get a national registry of asshats?

YOUNG LOVE

Jennifer came into the campground and seemed like a sweet young lady in her early twenties. She would be moving in with her much younger boyfriend who was a minor. It didn't occur to me at the time that that was statutory rape.

I met him, and he seemed okay. I didn't mind giving them a chance at the campground since she was employed, and his parents would be helping him with the rent.

Everything seemed okay that first day. Well, the morning was good, the afternoon was when it began. Okay, here we go... those next two weeks were so long.

That nice demeanor ended the minute they moved in. I've now learned that certain people think if they rent the site, they can do what they want, with no regard to neighbors, common sense and the rental contract.

Or maybe these two knuckleheads were just dicks that slipped under my radar by acting nice.

Their relationship had a strange dynamic, powered by mental illness, dependency, and drug use. I didn't know she was pregnant when they moved in.

What I could see was that he was under her thumb and if he voiced dissent, she would threaten to cut the baby out of her stomach, including when he took her drugs away from her. Yes, the authorities were called constantly. Yes, she threatened to cut her wrists unless he obeyed. They would each call 911 and hurl accusations as their rock and roll thundered through the park. Nobody got arrested, but the cops valiantly tried to keep the peace.

He wanted that baby badly; I think he thought the baby would solidify their relationship and perhaps tether her to him and tether him to the earth.

She was furious with me when I told her none of her friends were allowed on the property, but she was welcome to meet them at the entrance and socialize there. (Underage kids attempted to come over and flop.)

"Or" I told her reasonably, "You can go to their parents' homes to socialize."

I shouldn't have to remind y'all that it's pandemic times.

She Yelp reviewed the campground, and said it was terrible I wouldn't let her friends (druggies/homeless) into the park to socialize with her because she was almost bedridden during her pregnancy and didn't want to walk to the entrance of the campground to chat with her friends. It was all so unfair!

FYI, she was six weeks pregnant. The distance to the entrance of the park (it's not Jurassic Park) is two hundred feet.

I really wanted to reply on Yelp but held myself back from typing: *Well bitch, please, you sure could move your ass right outta the park when the cops found stolen guns and a cache of illegal drugs in your RV. You had no problem jogging off the property while the cops looked for you. Two cop cars took off after you. Any of that ring a bell?*

Wait, I'm getting ahead of myself.

So less than a full day on the property, the cops were called on their domestic dispute. The next day the same thing. The day after as well. The cops in town knew the young man very well. One cop said that everyone was waiting for him to turn eighteen so next time he committed a crime they could put him away for good. That news was an unpleasant surprise.

The younger boyfriend, the minor, Gunther, was troubled, to say the least, and his mother came every day to make sure he was on his meds. This I learned after they moved in. The mother hated Jennifer, but her son was so enamored of her and couldn't see her indifferent evil. Again, Gunther's mother came over daily to ensure he was on his meds, even though he was living with an adult who carried his child.

She was a good mother. Her devotion to her son was remarkable.

Cops were called, music was being played too loudly, cops were called, too many teenagers hanging around their RV. Lots of disturbing the peace calls to the cops.

Jennifer went to work at a local pancake house and left Gunther in the house to his own devices. I angered him when I kicked out friends who snuck onto the property to play pirated video games with him while missing home schooling because WE'RE IN THE MIDDLE OF A PANDEMIC WITH NO VACCINE IN SIGHT!

I understand that he's a man-boy, and lonely since he relied on friends and Jennifer to keep him grounded. This was not a good place for him. I wondered why he was not home with his family or online schooling during the day, but I understood that Jennifer was most likely using him for an unknown nefarious purpose. Also, he was so in love I doubt his mom could keep him home.

About day six, things got worse. I didn't know where Jennifer went, but Gunther was pacing the main road at the campground and shouting nonsense at passersby with his tightly coiled neck muscles bulging. I got a lot of frantic calls from tenants.

I went to his site and knocked on the wall of the RV. The front door was ajar, and music was pumping from the interior. I knocked harder. The interior of the RV was disgusting. Housekeeping was not their forte.

He came to the open door. I asked him politely to turn down the music. He obliged, then came back and began babbling. I couldn't follow anything, just snippets, and he was tensing and flexing, fists raised and then he rocked back and forth, and I stepped back myself because he seemed ready to propel himself right out the door and fly away. I didn't want to be in his way.

Something was seriously off with him.

I thanked him for lowering the volume, excused myself and hurried back to the office where I found his mother's number. I called and left messages, but I didn't get a call back. Christ, have I seen her stop by in the last day or so? Have I seen Jennifer?

I called the Sheriff's Department and asked them for a wellness check on a minor. I told them I thought Gunther was off his meds, and I was worried for him and the people around him. The dispatcher said she would relay the information to a deputy.

The deputy called and said he was extremely busy with more important emergencies. I reiterated that Gunther, a minor, seemed off his meds, I couldn't reach his mother, and his girlfriend was nowhere to be found and didn't answer her phone. The deputy said he'd swing by the campground and talk to him. I gave him Gunther's mom's number and Jennifer's. I don't know if he did stop by.

I went to bed that night troubled.

I think things quieted down a little, or maybe I wasn't paying much attention, but a couple of days after my interaction with Gunther, I was outside near the waste treatment plant at the back of the property. I heard numerous sirens and my camp host texted me and the text said, *get over to site 21*. I came up the lane, moved aside and watched the ambulance, paramedics, and police get close to the scene of the disaster.

Jennifer was not a witness to any of this madness; she arrived at the property ten minutes after the authorities. Maybe somebody let her know? Sent her a text?

Where had she been all this time?

Gunther relied on Jennifer to administer his meds since his mother was going to be out of town for five days. Jennifer decided to take off instead, without alerting anyone that the love of her life and the father of her unborn child would have no support from any caring adult for days.

Gunther, in his mania, broke out all the windows in the RV with his fists. He severed arteries and veins in both arms and blood splashed everywhere. Belongings tossed from the RV were coated with his blood.

As the paramedics tended to him, and the ambulance drivers were figuring out whether ER or ER and psych eval, I turned to the policeman and said, "This all could have been avoided. I called you guys days ago."

The officer looked at me, confused, "We never got a call on this."

I glanced at his vest camera. "We're on camera, correct?" He nodded.

"Check the call logs. Your department was notified. I asked for a wellness check earlier this week." I nodded toward Gunther, tightly tied down on a gurney, the hastily wrapped bandages on his hands were soaked through.

These cops are seriously overworked and overwhelmed, but having this earlier report fall through the cracks has led to this day.

No, that's not true. I doubt that the cops could have forced him to take his drugs; I don't think the law works that way. I accused the cops when it's not their fault. All that blood just freaked me out; it was everywhere.

The cops aren't to blame, the blame rested squarely on his girlfriend Jennifer. She knew his mom was out of town and she deliberately took off. Some people are just genuinely nasty. She should have known what would happen. I think she knew and simply didn't care.

Jennifer showed up at the conclusion of Gunther's macabre outdoor entertainment, most likely one of her friends at the **too many teenagers**' site alerted her, and she stood behind other tenants and watched the cops march into the RV.

I watched her, amazed that she hadn't paid any attention to Gunther; she made no attempt to approach while the paramedics worked on him. Instead, her gaze was intensely riveted on the cops inside the RV.

But then I knew why when the cops came out of the RV carrying rifles and plastic bags of what looked like drugs… I learned later that

Gunther told the police where to find the secret stash. It was hers, not his, and I believed he was trying to get her in trouble. If she were in jail, then she couldn't do drugs and hurt his baby.

For all her girth, she gracefully spun around and swiftly walked away. I followed. She stopped at the **too many teenagers'** site and whispered to one of the daughters. I told Jennifer to step away and go back to talk to the cops. The daughter at that site cussed me out and wept as her bestie scurried off the property and trotted south down the main highway.

I walked back up to the scene and told a cop Jennifer just took off.

Gunther's mother arrived and was speaking with the paramedics. I approached and she explained she'd been camping and out of cell range and why wasn't Jennifer taking care of him?

I gave her a minute and she calmed. She said that Gunther would be hospitalized first for self-inflicted injuries and then for his mental state.

I asked her to go in the RV and take all his belongings out. I said I would be removing the RV from the site. I asked, "You're his guardian, correct?" She nodded, "I am asking your permission to terminate this tenancy, okay?" She agreed and exited with a carload of his stuff pulled from that trashed RV.

I spent the rest of the afternoon hosing off the sprayed arterial blood all over the site and picked up the shards of glass, debris, and general trash that they had generated in a matter of days. Why gnawed on chicken wings and fast-food wrappers should be tossed into the fire pit is beyond me. I poured hydrogen peroxide on the graveled site, fire pit, picnic bench and the neighbor's windows and siding before again hosing them down.

I had a tow truck move the RV to the back of the property. Jennifer showed up a couple days later, in a complete snit because the site was empty, and her RV was by the dumpster. I told her she could pay the storage fees and remove it from the property. She said I was improperly evicting her. I told her to sue me.

It took a month of her trying to sneak onto the property to take belongings out, but she finally removed it. And no, she didn't pay the storage fees or past due rent, but she did get that disgusting blood-stained wreck off the property. Thank God, because it looked like a murder scene.

She probably moved it to her mother's driveway.

UNCHECKED MENTAL ISSUES

Malice and Barry

Middle-aged Malice and her boyfriend Barry were approved and moved in. I hadn't met the boyfriend upon moving in, just her. I never thought anything of it; you want to be on your own sir, thank you, it's appreciated.

One of the tenants casually knew Malice and said they had worked together at a market about two hours north and she was nice.

Based on that casual personal reference and the fact that nothing came up on the background check, I figured they would be a perfect, quiet couple to join the park's community.

So, about three weeks into this arrangement, I finally met him. He was frantically ding donging the office doorbell, which Pavlov's dogged me right off the couch in the adjacent house.

I came out on the porch and asked, "May I help you?" I didn't recognize him.

Barry, close to hysterical, said, "Malice has been abducted; she didn't come home." She was not wife, but his girlfriend.

"Okay, when did you see her last?"

He answered, "I've called and called, and she won't pick up." (I later I called and called and texted and emailed and she didn't pick up.)

"Okay, when did you see her last?"

"And Malice's applications for jobs is in the house, and-"

"Okay, when did you see her last?"

"And Diane said that the tank was loose." (Who is Diane?)

I spoke over his rambling, since he wouldn't answer my questions and he made no sense, "Okay, I'm calling the police to report a missing person." At this time, I suspected she was dead inside the RV, and he was trying hard to look crazy innocent. (I'd been watching a lot of murder shows.)

Later, I found out he was just crazy.

He screamed at me, "NO, DON'T DO THAT. THEY ARE CORRUPT AND MEAN, AND THEY TORE MY SHOULDER MUSCLE!"

What was he talking about?

I held out a hand like a traffic cop as he started to remove his shirt. "Sir, sir, please stop that. Stop that, don't, stop showing me your chest. Pull your shirt down! Stop that!"

Oh god, he had the physique of a burlap sack of warm lard. Everything was slowly moving south... just so melty, like he got all the gravity in the divorce.

He continued to shout at me while I tried to talk to that poor 911 dispatcher (we should be on a first name basis.)

That filthy shirt was now off one mottled-red tapioca shoulder. Yes, there was a faded crimson raised scar, but why was he showing me?

It was ludicrous for this guy to be so terrified his "wife" was missing but took the time to show me his disgusting body.

And who goes to their landlord to report their "wife" kidnapped and then screams to NOT call the police?

While he was barking like a famished seal, I loudly explained to the dispatcher the situation over his noises.

She asked, "Can you hand the phone to him?" Oh, God, he's gonna put his cooties all over my cell phone! Did I have to? Yes, because he wouldn't call them. Ugh.

Again, in hindsight, if he really thought his "wife" was missing, why was he talking to the campground manager? Why come to me? Why now use my phone to talk to the cops? It didn't make sense.

Lots of stuff I didn't *see* until much later.

It took all my resolve to gingerly hand my cell phone, MY cell phone, over to that babbling lardy mound of human.

He was not wearing a mask and was breathing all over my shit.

I cringed, mentally noting where the pandemic wipes were in the house. He talked for a half hour, and I couldn't leave because he had my phone pressed up tightly against his sweaty, oily face, and his filthy paws clutched my phone. I had things to do. I watched him with irritation from six feet away.

Finally, finally he finished, and said they will send out an officer. A *female* officer because he feared men. (That's what he told the dispatcher.)

He handed me my phone, and I took it with two fingers. He was still a-mumbling as I got back in my house and looked for the wipes.

Ugh, ugh. I threw up a little in my mouth. He smelled sooooooo bad, like body odor, and a butt that wasn't wiped properly for a long time.

I was wearing a mask, he was not.

A female officer arrived with a male backup who waited in the car, and she was stuck with Barry for two hours. I walked away to do chores, having already wasted time watching him cootify my phone.

I corralled several tenants who were outside enjoying the early morning sun and asked if they'd seen that Malice lady lately, and a few said they saw her walking off the property that morning with bags and thought maybe she was going into town to do laundry. I pondered that because they had a vehicle, so if it was laundry, she could have driven into town for that errand.

But if she wanted to leave without him knowing...

The officer and I spoke before she left (Barry was asked to go back to his RV because he wanted to hear what we were saying and was just getting too close).

As soon as he was out of earshot, like fifteen feet away but still watching us, all weirdly hunched over and neck craned forward like that extra three inches would help him hear us, I turned my back to him and told her quietly I thought his girlfriend ding dong ditched him and was not kidnapped. That whole kidnapping scenario rang false.

Just look at the scenario: they've been here less than a month from another town. She was spotted walking off the property with bags of belongings and told no one where she was going. This all smacks of domestic abuse, and she escaped.

The officer agreed and gave me her card and told me to call if he got weirder. She clearly saw there was something bizarre going on here.

Later that afternoon, after he continued to knock on doors asking people where his wife was, I called one of her friends on the application and asked her to call Malice.

She called me back a couple hours later, and said Malice texted her that she was safe and was not coming back.

I relayed that information to the officer, including the friend's number. The officer said she would confirm with the friend and then contact Barry and let him know Malice had simply broken up with him and walked away. Case closed.

But was it? Nope, it was just starting because Barry was sure that everyone knew a lot more than they were telling. How did I know that? Because *everyone* kept telling me he was going door to door on a search for Malice. I wasted a lot of time telling people that she dipped and was fine, no kidnapping.

This behavior is *after* he was notified by the authorities Malice was contacted and was safe and had left the premises. And him. Mainly him.

He was convinced there was an active, secret conspiracy to keep his "wife" from him, and he was going to find out all the facts and get that missing person's report reopened and the evil culprits arrested.

Barry focused on that distant, casual acquaintance of Malice's who lived in the park; they had worked together at a market and now Sam had become Barry's target of intense suspicion.

Sunday night at around 9:30 (this all started on a Tuesday) several ding dongs roused me. I dragged myself out of an edible induced coma and slipped into my house slippers and trudged outside. It was Sam, and he was royally pissed off. Barry had called the cops and demanded they immediately interrogate Sam on the whereabouts of his wife (girlfriend).

We walked up the roadway, me in my pjs, toward flashing lights. They wanted to ask Sam where Barry's "wife" went. Oh brother.

I identified myself to the handsome officer (there were a couple young ladies outside watching the excitement that was not Barry) and relayed the true details of Malice's departure while Barry paced and yelled in the cop car's headlights about his abducted wife (girlfriend).

The officer nodded in Barry's direction and said, "Yeah, I figured."

I wished him a nice evening, then walked over to Sam's RV. I said if Barry knocked on the RV, don't open the door and please call 911 immediately because Barry believed Sam was in on this conspiracy.

The only place this conspiracy was quickly gaining a foothold was in Barry's mind. She dipped out of this relationship, and he could not accept that fact.

Barry was actively disturbing every person he could reach with his wild stories and outlandish theories. How did I know? Because he didn't just go once to these sites, but many times.

Oh, and had potentially put their health at risk. Let's get to the gross part…

Malice and Barry had been here about three weeks, and they came in with an already defective RV. A couple of days before Malice's sudden departure, their full septic tank (black tank) literally unhooked itself from the RV and dropped to the ground, cracking and leaking sewage and toilet paper under the RV.

I told Malice it had to be cleaned up and fixed immediately because it was a health hazard. I told her to use the restrooms instead of her unit. She had codes to both the men's and women's restrooms.

Malice had nodded, as if she understood, but perhaps she was just nodding, thinking, *that's Barry's problem, isn't it? I'm dipping in a couple days. Dipping out with just a couple plastic bags of belongings.*

Now that Malice was gone, this was Barry's responsibility. I told him to get it pumped and reattached immediately.

The septic pumper was here that Sunday (8/1) but left empty handed. He stopped to speak with me—he couldn't pump it out and said it was beyond his pay grade. There was no way he could successfully pump it since all the liquids had seeped out the broken tank and the remaining solids inside had congealed. He doubted it could be reattached and suggested a new one be installed. I agreed.

This is fecal matter soaking into the ground

I immediately wrote to Barry that 1) the RV was uninhabitable and 2) it was a health hazard and 3) he needed to vacate the RV and move into a motel in town until it could be repaired. He refused to leave. He just said no.

He continued to use the toilet and flushed raw sewage onto the ground to the dismay and consternation of all the nearby neighbors.

After he received the notice from me, he ignored it. I just had to say this again because this was crazy making; what sane person believed that flushing raw sewage onto the ground is a good idea?

I called the community mental health department and filed an elder abuse report in that Barry needed help. I explained he was unable to function to keep himself and others safe. I called the Environmental Health Department to report the discharge of raw sewage, and I called the police and said that the single women on either side of him are now afraid to come outside their homes, because the minute they do, he was on them like white on rice, perhaps looking for a replacement.

They couldn't go outside without that intrusive sack of body odor and entitlement skipping into their sites to start unwelcome conversations. One said he left some crap (not literally, although that does come up later) on her picnic table, and I told her to throw it away. She said she was afraid to, so I did it. He was frightening them.

I told her if he accused her, to tell him I did it. Go ahead, get mad at me.

Get in line.

After all the calls and reports filed, I waited for somebody in a position of power to red tag that RV, get him in a motel, off the property and onto suitable meds, so that I can 1) get the RV repair guy out to properly sever the broken tank and attach a new one; 2) get a tow guy out to tow it to storage area so that I can clean the ground below and remediate the area and 3) assure the other 80 people living here that he is a bizarre mental health anomaly and that this place is safe for all.

This is just so not right.

I asked him to get rid of this toxic waste once that tank was severed from the RV (which still had an open pipe flushing sewage on
the ground). He ignored me.

It must have been an extremely abusive relationship for Malice
to leave with mere bags of belongings. She walked off the property
and left me with this aggressive nutcase who hated me with a passion
bordering on what? What's after insane? He didn't even know me but
needed someplace to focus all that stored up aggression. He was so
angry at her for leaving. If he kept it inside, he'd probably just blow,
like that dead whale they loaded with explosives on an Oregon beach.

He didn't want to be here as he had told me numerous times, yet
he refused to leave. He hated it here, that's all I heard. I don't get it…

I understand why she did it, perhaps this was the only way to
get free of this malignant limpet, but she didn't think it through, or
didn't care, that I would be left holding this bag of flaming shit.

The attorney worked on the eviction notice and I waited for him to mail it over. Once that was served it would still be an additional thirty-five days of him here—days that would be filled by constant harassment of others, the continued nonsense of his conspiracy theories and other obnoxious behavior.

His sense of entitlement was incredible. What gave him the right to repeatedly go door to door at all hours—never mind his neighbor who worked the night shift, or the other one who just got home from the lumber mill—asking what they knew about his "wife's" abduction.

Then top that off with his site filled with fecal matter; the wafting stench was indescribable and that's coming from someone who works in a waste treatment plant.

All that shit was something I would tidy up after he finally left. That was a growing party favor for me at the end of this soiree.

Did you know Covid exists in poop?

DEQ arrived, looked at the mess and did nothing; the Environmental Health Department didn't show up. I learned that there was no law on the books besides "illegal dumping" which wouldn't cover what he was doing. Thanks, guys.

The Veterans Admin guys who were called said they can't help because he refused any help, and they were not sure if he was a vet. The community mental health center... they also couldn't do anything because he refused help.

If you're mentally ill and refuse offered help, there is nothing anybody can do about it.

This was all simply terrifying and completely out of my wheelhouse.

Since Thursday, 8/6/21, he had been repeatedly told to keep his distance from me because I recognized abusive, controlling behavior and there was no reason for him to even talk to me.

No matter how many times I told him she had dipped, she was gone, don't talk nonsense, go away and clean up your site, you smell like shit… he just kept moving closer, his angry, dirty face twisted with incomprehensible rage. It was awful.

It's like when you hold your breath against something disgusting, but after you move away, that horrid odor is now lodged in your sinuses, like it scampered up your nostrils and set up camp.

There were Barry cooties everywhere.

When Malice was here, I never saw him out of the trailer; since his punching bag walked, he was looking for a substitute and had focused his rage on me.

Again, let me reiterate for the nth time: the pandemic was raging with no vaccine in sight, and I was trying to run a RV park and keep people safe. I cleaned the restrooms daily, mowed, did my chores in the waste treatment plant, and cared for the animals. I'm busy, okay?

But this skanky knucklehead thought he could pester and badger me daily, even when I said, "GET AWAY FROM ME!"

The worst part was he could see the repulsion and horror on my face, and I think he liked it.

I walked the goats over to the dog park for recess and was cleaning out the goat pens on the far west side of the 6.5-acre property. One of the male tenants chatted with me while I shoveled scat.

From my vantage point, I watched the Veteran's Admin guy as he drove away from Barry's site. This was not his first, or second visit. Barry now looked for another target, scanned the area, saw me, and approached as inexorably as the blob. I told him to stop when he was twenty feet away. He didn't. He was always trying to get closer to me than he should. He was doing that man thing where they want to bully you with their size, and he was sizable (super fat).

I was wearing a mask, he was not.

He mumbled some complaint about how I was not helping, how no one was helping (remember, I just updated you that he refused help from *two* separate governmental agencies) and I told him to just pay rent.

He said, "No, I'm not going to pay rent."

Okay, whatever. I then told him in a stern voice, "Go away," because I did not want to communicate with him, but instead he edged closer. I backed up, still holding my pitchfork, but now I've leveled it at him.

I could smell him above the goat scat. My skin crawled.

The male tenant watching said, "Man, back up."

Barry then swiveled those numerous chins and focused his ire on him and accused, "You know where she is, don't you?"

The tenant shook his head. Everybody knew about this ongoing delusion; Barry just could not fathom how she got away from him. Everyone at the park had learned of his delusions; he delivered his fantasies daily door to door.

I said, "If you don't go back to your RV, I'm calling 911."

He continued to edge closer.

This was insane! I was his landlord of less than two months! What the hell did he want from me!

I called 911 again and asked for an officer. There was now a huge running tally of 911 calls since his girlfriend noped outta here.

He watched me make the call. What was wrong with him? I know I kept saying that, but I was so puzzled. This daily onslaught, this barrage of revolting behavior was so over the top and continuous—every day the same abhorrent acts.

He backed off, and I took my pitchfork with me to the house (something I've never done before). The Veteran's guy was talking with the camp host near the entrance of the property, so he hadn't left yet. I approached and they went silent, probably wondered why I had a pitchfork, and I relayed what had happened, and he said he couldn't help since Barry refused help and doubted he was even a veteran.

At that moment, the Veteran's guy answered his phone. It was Barry calling him to come back because he wanted to tell him about what just happened (me calling 911).

The Veteran's guy sighed and headed back to Barry's site. I went to the office and checked the mail. The eviction notice for Barry arrived!

My camp host and I walked up (my pitchfork left leaning against the front of the house), eviction in hand. The Veteran's guy was still there, thank God, and the camp host served the notice. I felt safer in that Barry most likely wouldn't get violent or threatening with the man from the Veteran's Administration at his site. I was correct; he merely accepted the notice. I know it would have been a vastly different scenario if we had no male backup.

The cop called me back from my earlier 911 call and said to file a stalking restraining order. When that restraining order was in effect, then he and other cops would be able to *do* something.

Malice and Barry were here starting 6/26, she bounced around 7/26 and by Saturday 8/7 I had wasted HOURS trying to help this guy. To my dismay, he refused to pay for repairs and refused all help.

Let's reiterate: The government agencies that have been contacted and cannot assist in any fruitful manner are the following: The Community Mental Health Agency, the Disabled Elderly Agency, the Environmental Health Agency, the Code Enforcement Division of Law Enforcement, the Veterans Administration, and the Department of Environmental Quality.

I felt alone.

I was stuck with this disgusting person until I could get him evicted. I had at least 35 days with him, and perhaps longer if he wouldn't leave by that date. *Damn, damn.*

Once in the house, I locked the door, which I never did during the middle of the day and completed the stalking restraining order forms. I printed all the documents and then ventured out and finished my chores while looking over my shoulder the entire time. I was waiting for him to slowly pursue me to pick a fight I was not invested in and just didn't care about. It was a horrid feeling.

Dude, stay in your lane.

Malice was very much on his mind. He could not accept that she willingly left him, she had to have been kidnapped. His mantra continued to be that he had saved her, and I knew he felt cheated, because she *owed* him.

His fragile ego denied reality and created a scenario of kidnapping instead of the simple truth that she walked.

Half of what he said was to provoke me. He was a stranger, our relationship was merely landlord- tenant for mere weeks, and yet he kept snarling at me repeatedly, daily, every chance he got, "You are not treating me with respect."

What was there to respect? You didn't pay rent, you terrorized the park by knocking on doors at all hours, you harassed the women on either side of you, and wait, the cherry on top is that you pooped on the ground!

I didn't respect you? You're right, you're a malevolent asshat. Nobody liked you, and I doubt anyone ever did. If you had any redeeming qualities, they suffocated under the massive weight of your narcissist sociopathic entitlement.

Friday morning, I filed the stalking restraining order with the court. The hearing date was Monday, 8/9/21.

Back at the park I worked on the waste treatment plant then walked to the office. I rounded the corner and dammit, Barry sat there in his filthy white tennis outfit on my NEW CUSHIONS in a chair right outside the office.

Mary, a longtime tenant, was talking to him, but stopped when she saw my face, instantly knew something was wrong and glanced at Barry.

I skidded to a stop and backed up. "What do you want?"

Barry pulled out a wad of cash from his back pocket. OMG, his hands and clothes were filthy, the cooties were crawling everywhere. "I want to pay rent," he said.

Recall yesterday he refused to pay...

"Just stay there," I ordered. He stood and I backed up. "You are **not** coming in the office; you will stay out here." There is only one way into and out of the office.

He looked at Mary, stopped and handed me the cash.

I went into the office, locked the door behind me, and came out with his receipt, hands smelling of Purell. Mary had left and I walked by him to the house and dropped the receipt on the coffee table in front of him.

In a demanding, petulant voice laden with barely suppressed rage that screamed softly, *I'm so mad at you I can hardly stand it, I'm being as polite as I can manage, but I'd really rather enjoy hurting you,* Barry said, "So what is the update on getting my RV fixed?"

I looked at him, stunned, the hairs on my neck standing at attention. I replied coldly and hoped my voice didn't tremble, "I'm done helping you; you are on your own."

See, I tried to be as helpful as I could within limits, and since I wanted him gone, I've been talking to my RV repair guy and he was the one who severed the black tank which should have had Barry using the restroom, but no, Barry still flushed his toilet onto the ground. The RV repair guy told him to take that tank to the dumpster, but Barry refused, and there it sat, stinking up the site.

After the confrontation at the goat pens yesterday, I've had it. That broken, leaking black tank was his personal property and I was not raising a further finger.

Let me repeat—he had the men's bathroom code from day one.

He headed back to his RV and later that day, I learned the mental health woman was coming back with the Veteran's guy as her backup. On her way out, she notified me that again, he refused assistance.

These helpful agency people were very concerned, but their hands were tied; they couldn't help someone who wouldn't accept help.

One would think there'd be a law for these kinds of people in that medical care and intervention should be available even against their will, but I understand that was a slippery and potentially dangerous slope.

Once they left, he sat his bulk down twenty feet from my front door, turning the chair to face my home's entrance. I came outside and told him he was not allowed to sit there, and he must return to his RV.

He refused to do so, and I was not comfortable walking by him to get to the office and he knew it. He deliberately did this and enjoyed it. I didn't know what he'd do; I sensed that violent undertone, that barely repressed fury.

He was mad at Malice, but I was convenient. Once again, it was not my fault that she dipped. I had trouble understanding why he focused on me—I was his landlord, that's it and had done zero to encourage his behavior which only confirmed my opinion of him as an abuser of women.

Malice, girl, I feel you.

The restraining order had been filed. The hearing was Monday, but he had not yet been served as I told him to move away from the office and go back to his site. He would not go. I told him I was going to call 911 to remove him. He said, "I'll wait."

Okay. I apologized to the dispatcher and said, "Hey, it's Rondi." She said, "Is it Barry?" They will send someone out. All of this was being said on my porch as I watched him watch me.

He left before the cops got there.

When the cop arrived, I told him about the hearing on Monday.

He drove up and spoke to Barry at his site and returned to me. The cop said he warned him to stay away from the office and me and did not tell him about the restraining order. The cop didn't want to set him off. That was reassuring. Even the cop recognized how dangerous Barry had become.

The weekend was quiet, but I paid careful attention to my surroundings and made sure my doors were locked.

I was so frustrated. Why did I have to be on red alert? Why was this horrid man disrupting my life? I hated having to look both ways.

It was an awful feeling, a nauseous trepidation. I felt hunted.

In court on Monday, the first hearing was a woman crying her eyes out. It was her sixth meth hearing. This time, she got probation, but was forbidden to see her daughter for a year. The reason? They did meth together and while the mother was trying to get clean, the daughter was not. Very sad.

Next, it was my turn. The judge granted the temporary restraining order and announced that it would be served on Wednesday.

Once he was served, he could either ignore it and the permanent restraining order would be granted *or...* he could fight it. There was a further court date to set trial if he fought the temporary stalking restraining order or to have the order granted.

The temporary restraining order was served on him by the cops. The order continued until 8/24/21 which was the next hearing.

During that period, under the temporary restraining order, he only attempted to talk to me once, but I busily shunned him and walked away.

Had he tried to follow, I would have liberally pepper sprayed him, and then called 911.

I only saw Barry in passing while I was doing chores that he came to the office, found his mail on the counter, and left.

When I went down to the office, there was an upended bag of shit on the welcome mat outside the office door. I don't know if it belonged to a dog or human, but I was pretty sure it was from Barry.

This dude had a shit fixation, and continued to flush everything onto the ground. Remember, he had the men's bathroom code, which makes this all the worse.

This was a purposeful torment. Tenants continued to complain about the stench, and I continued to say to call the health department to report him. I knew there was not much they could do, but I wanted a paperwork trail showing how many people he had affected.

I had dealt with a gamut of impaired, drunk, disabled, depressive, troubled, addicted, delusional, violent, abusive, mentally ill individuals before, but *never* had anyone like this. He made it *personal.*

One of the tenants told me that Barry continued to share to everyone he saved Malice from an abusive boyfriend... *he saved her.*

Oh boy, that sounded like a relationship built on mutual respect and an emotional even footing. Everything he did leaned toward domestic abuse and a deep abiding hatred of women.

Wait! This monster saved her from another monster?

The hearing on 8/24/21 was quick and weird.

I was there to get the legal means to keep this creep away from me; he was there because that's who he was.

Barry was in court to contest a restraining order on property where he'd been served an eviction notice by a landlord who had known of his existence for under two months.

We were the only ones there; all the other cases were Webex'd since the Covid cases in town were skyrocketing. The court didn't have an email for Barry, thus the in-person hearing.

Barry "couldn't" wear a mask, so he was put in a jury room and given a laptop. Let me tell you, he was not up on technology. How hard was it to sit in front of the laptop with Webex and reply when you were spoken to?

The judge asked me if I wanted the restraining order on a permanent basis, and I nodded. The judge looked at me and I said, "Yes, I want a permanent restraining order." I guess I needed to say it aloud for the court record. Nods don't count.

Barry contested that and said he wanted a trial. I should have expected that, but it still caught me by surprise. *Like, seriously?*

Let's recall that he had been on the property for *less than two months*; he was served with eviction papers to get out by 9/7/21, so why was he even interested in this order?

Because he was the guy who made everything difficult for everybody. He was the Debbie Downer at every party. He was literally the dude who pooped on his site without a septic tank and wondered why people hated him.

He was the guy who ran out of dog food for days.

The judge asked me regarding witnesses, and I said, "two to three."

The judge asked Barry the same question, and Barry replied with a question, "When is she doing the lie detector?"

The judge glanced at me; I remained motionless behind my mask.

"Uh, there will be no lie detector tests administered, sir, and in any event, they are inadmissible," the judge replied.

Barry said, "I have two witnesses, me, and my girlfr—" He tapered off the end of that sentence.

Recall that Barry went mental *after* the girlfriend exited.

"I have an email," he continued.

Well, that evidence would break this case wide open—an email from someone, not me, because I didn't have his email.

The hearing was set for 9/2/21 for the final countdown. Barry was escorted out first by the Sheriff to get his papers and then to give them an email for the Webex hearing.

Finally, the officer escorted me out of the courtroom, the officer by my side quietly said, "I need to walk you out; he's in his car staring at the entrance." He had been in his car waiting to like, what, scare me? Christ, can I waste any more of my precious time on Earth? What a doofus.

Out the open front doors of the courthouse, I saw him glaring behind his windshield and heard his dog barking. That inconsiderate asshat left his dog in the car this entire time. Christ.

I got in my car (that was three slots away), thanked the deputy, and went to the Sheriff's department to get the 911 call log. I wanted the judge to see what I have been dealing with over these past several weeks. I imagined there were close to a dozen 911 Barry calls during that period.

I also reattached the two pepper sprays to my keys that I couldn't take inside the courthouse.

I looked in my rear-view mirror, but he wasn't following. I smiled and thought it would be hilarious if he stalked me to the 911 dispatch offices. I wouldn't have to call them; I could just walk in and point over my shoulder at Barry.

Later that day, I was getting ready to fly south for a few days to work at my other job and see my family. I managed the waste treatment plant and sampled, fed the animals, and tidied up. While I was running around getting things done, this asshat pulled up to the dog park (He had never used it before. He knew I dropped the goats off every morning for a couple hours to stretch their legs when most people were at work and not needing the park) and was blocking the park entrance with his vehicle.

He was dragging that poor underfed dog into the park by the scruff of its neck. Where was his leash?

He was now twenty feet from the office. I started filming and told him he was being filmed, and I was calling the police. I took two videos at that time showing what he was doing and the distance. He finally got the dog back in his car and took off, but guess what? Thirty seconds later, he came back and was wandering around the office area, loitering. So, I took another video. Dammit, I had better things to do.

He shouldn't have been up at the office. His mail, if any (never), would be under a small white plastic basket on a table in the entryway. This meant all he had to do was drive by, see if it was empty or not, and then if there was any mail, stop, open his door, grab it, and continue. But no... he got out of his car and started to walk about while I was recording him.

He was enjoying this.

I absolutely hated how much real estate he was sitting on in my brain.

He was mayhem in a pasty, lard filled meat suit.

And the stench surrounding him, and his site was, geez. He made repulsion a physical expression, a revulsion quite like the unexpected smell of decay and rot and the hum of maggots as your shoe barely misses week old roadkill.

The interior of his RV reeked through the perpetually open door, and now he did as well. The smell marinated into his large, blackhead filled greasy pores and extruded from his constant film of sweat (it was 66 Fahrenheit).

He wore the same outfit for days on end—grimy shorts, t-shirt, and flip flops. His toenails looked like the neglected nails of an elderly man. They were yellow, thick, and surrounded by calluses... and filth... and fungus. They were also LONG and tapered at the ends like talons of a gargoyle.

Finally, he was gone from the area. I called the cops and said I needed to show him the video, in light of the restraining order. The cop showed up and said to send it to him, and he'd forward it to the district attorney.

He also mentioned that Barry called 911 to report me videotaping him. I shook my head. It was just not the same.

He was calling the police on *me*. The funny thing was all he had to do was leave. Just get out. There were numerous RV parks all over the state. He and Malice were at one before; go back, asshat.

He literally had been here since 6/26/21, and it was now 8/27/21. Two months... but it felt like years.

There was no reason he should want to stay since everyone hated him. He whined that no one would talk to him.

One of my tenants said he was in the men's restroom and Barry came out of the stall, approached him at the urinal and said, "How come nobody likes me?"

Right there, right there, pal... you didn't even wash your hands and yet you crowded the guy at the urinals with his zipper down and asked why you aren't popular?

Dude, you've been flushing sewage on the ground for over a month, polluting the world, harassing everyone with your madness and you think that doesn't depress your popularity?

Dude, you leave your RV door open and scream and yell and play loud music all night and you think that makes friends?

How could he think anyone enjoyed his existence?

Okay, time to travel, peace out. I did enjoy the drive to the airport. I listened to the podcast, Morbid, and made sure the doors were locked and windows were up. I love their line, "Fresh air is for dead people."

Because it's true.

Finally, I arrived in Southern California. I looked at my park cameras and saw the woman who lived next to him at my door at 9:30 that night.

I emailed her asking what's up. She said that this was the second night he had been screaming and shouting and singing and slamming things in his RV. She had called 911 and reported him.

I thanked her and said to keep me posted.

Whilst I was down in Southern California, the camp host texted me that asshat Barry stopped by to apologize for his behavior and asked if she forgave him.

Yesterday, he gave her five hearty fuck yous at the top of his lungs and today he was sorry?

Camp host smartly replied if he got out before the court hearing on Thursday, she would forgive him.

During that same weekend while I was gone (but not gone at all because of phone calls and emails), he took his dog into the chicken coop to terrorize my baby chickens; he allowed his dog to scare the goats, unleashed and running at them while they were in their pens, making them frantic, and to top it off, had his unleashed mutt attack a woman's service dog.

All in a day's work for a shitheel. I told everybody to call 911 and report him.

Now animal control was involved, and a case opened. If you serve an asshat with an eviction notice, he will weaponize his pet. So even though I was out of town at my other job, I was still at work there. Thanks Barry, ever so much.

Back in town, I stopped by the Sheriff's Department to pick up the 911 call log. I took it to the county courthouse and brought it to the clerk's window to file a copy with the paperwork for the stalking restraining order hearing, and then I got an unpleasant surprise.

The clerk told me I needed to give Barry a copy of the document I filed with the court; I had expected the clerk to email/mail him a copy, but no, they don't do that.

I would have to deliver to Barry a copy of the 911 call log that I wanted introduced at the hearing that was for a stalking restraining order to keep him away from me.

Did that make any sense? In a safety kind of way?

Dammit, you'd think in a restraining order hearing they wouldn't force the person asking for the order to keep him away to mandate contact with the guy.

I made a copy, gave it to the camp host, and walked with her to his site. I was not going to go alone.

She banged on his open door and tried to hand it to him when he appeared from the dark interior, but he refused to take it and started an argument with her. She put it on the picnic table and turned to leave as his dog rushed out the door and jumped on her back.

It was not genuinely vicious; it was just incredibly untrained and unmanageable. She kicked at it, and it turned and jumped on me. I pushed it off twice, I kicked it off a third time.

All the while, Barry just stood in the doorway and watched. He made absolutely no effort to rein in his dog.

I kicked it again, and then pepper sprayed its face. That didn't seem to slow it down, and it ran down the road, looking for trouble. I followed, and when it got to the woman's house with the service dog and climbed up the steps, I sprayed it again to get it away from her door.

It still didn't slow down; it ran farther down the road and turned into the camp host's site with her two very well-behaved German Shepherds on leads. I sprayed it again, and it finally backed up.

I glanced up the road; Barry was at his site and was yelling.

Camp host and I stayed at her site while we heard him shouting about assault, lie detector tests, and some batshit threats.

Camp host yelled, "Hose down your dog's face you idiot!"

But he didn't… he just continued to babble while the dog trotted up the road and circled him. He couldn't comprehend that his dog was uncomfortable—nothing existed but his imaginary victimhood.

I felt sorry for the dog, but I didn't have a choice. I was healing from two recent spinal surgeries. If I got hurt, everything would fall apart.

The camp host called 911 and relayed what had happened, and I went back to the waste treatment plant to finish processing some shit.

My other office. Yes, what's in those tanks is what you think. I turn influent into almost potable effluent. Almost...

I was running a backwash of the filtration system in the waste treatment plant. Once I finished that, I came out to find the woman whose service dog was attacked over the weekend waiting for me.

We spoke and I heard the camp host yell something. I looked up toward the office about two hundred feet away and Barry stood there, staring at me and shouting into his phone.

He just wouldn't stop.

The camp host wielded a small baseball bat and shouted at him to get lost.

Instead of retreating to his RV, he entered the public bathroom.

Barry was in the bathroom calling the police on both the camp host and me for felony assault. On his dog. I could hear him shouting behind the closed restroom door.

When he came out of the restroom and returned to his site, I was already donning my mask and gloves. I had Lysol at the ready.

It was disgusting—he had been spitting all over the bathroom sink and faucet handles. I almost puked as I sprayed the entire area—liberally—with disinfectant.

Why wasn't he taking care of his dog? Why was he following me, and then going into the restroom? Just to spit all over everything. Good lord.

As I was finishing up cleaning the men's restroom, the sheriff showed up. The camp host and I explained the situation.

He sighed and drove down the road. I cleaned the women's restroom since I was still dressed for the occasion.

As the sheriff was leaving, I waved him down. He said, "I told him I'm not going to cite you or your camp host for anything. His dog was off leash and out of control, and I was here for the attack on the service dog last weekend. You had a right to spray that dog. He said some other crazy stuff, but that's mostly it."

I thanked him and went back to chores and decided to leave the goats in their pens. I was worried he might run them down in his car if he was really heading deeper into psychosis or whatever mental condition he had.

I prepared for the court hearing. I had the 911 call log and was ready to lay out the last two months in the briefest manner. Being as OCD as I am, I of course typed up everything double spaced like I was getting ready to present my fifth-grade report on Abraham Lincoln.

Thursday rolled around and I rounded up my masked witnesses in the house along with the paperwork, and then signed into Webex. We waited, muted.

It was the first time I had anyone in the house since the pandemic began. This was months before the vaccine was available. I was scared and anxious and felt crawly. We were too close to each other for the zoom meeting!

The judge entered, but no Barry. So, we waited, and it was now twenty minutes past the hearing time. The judge then granted the permanent (indefinite) stalking restraining order.

Later that morning, I went to the clerk's office to get a copy. They would mail Barry his. Good, because I'm not going to his site to drop it off. I was glad I prepared like it was for a final, but I should have known he wouldn't show.

What was his defense against a permanent restraining order? If he just left, it would have been dismissed/revoked by me. But he just wouldn't leave.

The very next day, he let his dog off leash and again, it went after the woman's service dog. The cops were called by the woman. Barry also called, and he was rambling away on his cell as he shambled down to the restroom, dog in tow (finally leashed).

Please recall, at the beginning of this mess, Barry was terrified of the cops, and I had to call to report Malice missing. Now look at how far he's come.

He took a shower with his dog, and I'm not even gonna start about health code violations to a guy who shits on the ground.

I had gone up to the service dog woman's site and was waiting for the cops with her. The cop showed up, and boy was he pissed. At me. He said that I deliberately antagonized Barry. I just stared and shook my head.

He continued, "He said you broke into his house to give him the court documents."

Wait a minute! Why are you listening to Barry?

"Sir, yesterday, I had to serve him with the exhibits for the hearing since the court clerk wouldn't do it; I had the camp host hand it to him. He started the scene by letting his dog out. You think anyone here would go inside his house? I have a permanent stalking restraining order against him issued by the Judge."

The tenants around me listened and said nothing. The cop was furious, and I didn't know why.

"Did you have to kick his dog and spray it with pepper spray?" the cop said accusingly.

"Yes, yes, I did." I told him again what happened.

And was *still* happening. Because you, officer, were here on a call regarding another attack on a service dog by that very same dog.

"Was it vicious?"

I answered truthfully, "How would I know? It wouldn't stop jumping on me and it's over 80 pounds and I kicked it, and when that didn't work, I sprayed it."

My question is why is that dog being weaponized without consequences?

Why are we back on this saga? The cop yesterday didn't have a problem, but this one was butthurt that I didn't stand there and let a strange dog hurt me.

Seriously, the notion of falling on my back scares me and my tailbone. I'm held together by zip ties. At least that's what they look like on the MRI.

Lord knows what kind of nonsense Barry nonstop mumbled into this cop's ear but when the cop blurted, "Why can't you guys be nice to him?" I was simply flabbergasted.

Then I got it. He felt sorry for Barry! He knew nobody liked him and he was an outcast. The cop hadn't considered anything but poor Barry's feelings. OMG, this cop must have had a hard time in high school and held onto that resentment. Was that the trigger for his anger?

At that point, there were five people congregated in the group as he lectured, "Why can't you say hi, and how are you?" Oh, geez, the cop is taking this personally!

I knew the cop found the ensuing silence deafening.

None of us spoke or volunteered to do so. Did he not know these folks had to smell his feces for a month plus?

That Barry was up at all hours screaming, yelling, and singing with his front door wide open?

I could go on, but it was getting defensive out here and I didn't need to change this one cop's mind.

This cop pleaded for everyone to play nice with this asshat. This was ridiculous, insulting, and demeaning. Also, it was worrisome.

You couldn't make me. You are not the boss of me. And I was finished placating an abuser.

Barry was upset because no one liked him. And this cop was chastising us! How dare you!

Sir, if Barry doesn't like it, he could MOVE!

The cop said, "He's so mad. I don't know what he'll do."

I almost replied, "So, instead of citing Barry for his dog's behavior, you want us to play nice with him so as not to upset him?"

Before I had a chance, he pivoted, leaped, and swan dived into ridiculousness. He had the gall to state with a straight face that since this was private property, the city and county rules on leashes don't apply. Thus, Barry didn't break any laws.

Really? I could tell he was making it up just to book off the property. He showed surprise, as if he couldn't believe he said what he said. It was so beyond stupid. My mouth was open, aghast.

I stood with five other people listening to this cop. None of us said anything because it was ludicrous to reply or argue.

So, I could have my own hunting party and kill tenants who don't pick up their dogs' poops? Was I a sovereign nation? Why didn't anyone tell me sooner?

This book would have certainly taken a darker turn had I known there were no laws on private property.

Why was I wasting dollars on lawyers when I could use lethal force?

I'd be *Putin* my troubles away.

Officer, sir, don't demand that I, the landlord, be nice to a two-month tenant who's not only been served with eviction papers but was also under a permanent stalking restraining order.

It concerned me if this cop ever went on domestic calls what misogynistic advice he would impart to the victim.

I turned and walked down the road. What a bullshit waste of time, dealing with a cop who felt sorry for disgusting Barry.

Later in the afternoon, a local repairman came by and severed Barry's sewer pipe leading to nowhere but gravel and installed a shorter pvc pipe. He told Barry to use the restrooms until Barry bought a new black tank to install. He also worked on Barry's vehicle, so everything was ready to roll.

Barry had money, but he just chose not to pay. Now that the RV wasn't dragging a container of poop and his vehicle was in working order, he could leave at any time. *Any time. Any time.*

The next day, it was quiet, thank God. It was a beautiful day with just a hint of fall in the air. I mowed and got my cardio in. The aspens shivered in the breeze, leaves gently falling. The broad sky's gigantic fluffy clouds raced by. The goats were fed and happy, what a great—

Oh, crap.

Sam came over and was shaken and very pale. He said Barry, after yesterday's drama of Barry's dog attacking his mother's service animal, Barry's cursing, the hatred, the vitriol hissed at him all day yesterday and now… *just* now, Sam said, in a tone best used for when one was in awe of a double rainbow, that Barry once again entered his site, banged repeatedly on his door, and then asked him to…

help him reopen the police's missing person's case on Malice and add all the things he must know.

That was terrifying on so many levels.

This was like *Shutter Island*, but with more e-coli.

Barry had literally taken a huge step back in time. He just couldn't stop this fantastic, incredible theme running in that rattle trap noggin.

He could not accept that she left him because that would mean… okay, he's *Shutter Island*. He could not fathom the truth of their relationship. She must have been kidnapped. He saved her, for Christ sakes!

The way she dumped him here gave her a head start, but he wouldn't give up. She had disappeared, and her friend said she was safe. End of story.

I was shell shocked to consider that this guy was truly insane. I mean, he was nuts, but this was super, duper scary.

I told Sam to keep his door locked, and to not engage.

I was back at the house, checking emails, and lo and behold, Malice had sent me three emails today with no content. Barry was fishing and must have unlocked her email account, but I was sure she had a new one.

For a moment, for a dangerous, stupidly reckless moment, I wanted so badly to type, "Malice, why are you using this old email?

Why aren't you using the new one? Do you want me to call on your new number?"

Of course, caution prevailed, because he would have stalked his way to my door and demanded information, restraining order or not.

I knew for sure he was the one who was using Malice's email address, but that confirmation was not worth the risk... although, it would have been funny....

Sam contacted me a day later and said Barry had again waited outside his RV and asked again if they could start working on the new police report now.

He was trying super hard to create a folie a deux—but no one wanted to join in his reindeer games.

I loaned Sam a pink container of pepper spray and told him to be careful since Barry was now seriously wandering into lunacy.

In the afternoon, a gloriously sunny day, one of the tenants ding-donged and said that there was a "boom" noise coming from Barry's site, and that the guy tore up an American flag and dumped it into the fire pit. I told him that if he was worried, he needed to call 911 to alert the authorities.

Seriously, adults, why were you coming to me? Call 911.

After the response of that last cop, I was taking a step back; somehow, that cop wanted me to NOT do my job of managing the campground. Was the restraining order for Barry or for me? Because I felt hobbled at this point. Let the tenants call in the alarm.

In the evening, two tenants complained of Barry banging and yelling all night, and I said to call 911.

In the morning, while at the office taking rent payments, Richard stepped up with a flag in his arms and said he found it in the fire pit in site #21 and he was livid; he was a veteran and proud of his service, as he should be. Thank you, Richard, for your service.

Originally, that flag was in a shadow box. Barry kept telling everyone that he was a veteran, but I doubted it. The Veterans admin said they weren't sure, and Barry told the officer that the flag was his father's. That made more sense as we were close in age, and my father (Korea) and grandfather (WWII) served.

Barry destroyed that shadow box and was getting ready to burn his father's flag. First it was his, then his father's, and now it was in the fire pit. That should tell you a lot about him...

Richard handed me the flag, and I said I would retire it respectfully. My camp host was enjoying a bonfire in the meadow, and I asked her if the fire was large and hot enough to burn the flag completely.

She said it was, and I handed it to her. If you're wondering about the proper disposal protocol for a flag, just google it. This flag was dirtied, stained, and had obviously been mistreated. Barry was waiting for somebody to interact with him since everyone had been shunning him and what better way to garner attention than to trash the American flag in a park full of veterans?

I went back to mowing the meadow. A tenant came over and said that Barry had been destroying the picnic table all night and that I'd better go look. Of course...

Crap, crap, crap. I was trying to stay away from this dork.

The fun never ends.

I called the non-emergency sheriff line and explained I wanted him cited for criminal mischief. My resolution to *not* call the authorities lasted a hot minute.

I went back to mowing.

I know I bring up mowing a lot, but there's six acres of freaking grass and it grows so fast.

About an hour later, a sheriff showed up and I saw him talking to Barry. Poor sheriff was there for an hour.

Relaying all the shenanigans took Barry some time. I finished the meadow and went inside the house for a cool drink.

It was almost fall, but it was warm. Seventy-two degrees with the vast sky a blue that was hard to describe… robin's egg?

It was weird too. During the pandemic, not seeing contrails in the sky, so many flights canceled.

The sheriff knocked, and I came out with my mask on for a chat. He explained some of the usual Barry nonsense and I said, "Talk to the sergeant, she knows the scoop." He laughed and said he was backup for that first day so many moons ago. I laughed too; it seemed like an eternity.

Time had been strange since the pandemic, but that day so long, long ago was like four, five weeks? How?

He said that Barry destroyed the picnic bench in retaliation because someone stole his flag.

I swiftly corrected that bullshit, and explained the flag was dumped in the fire pit and Richard retrieved it. He gave me the flag around 3:00 p.m. while the destruction of the picnic bench started the night before.

These two events were mutually exclusive, and there was no causal relationship.

Barry obviously wanted an excuse to destroy my shit. There was no excuse.

The officer asked if I wanted a citation issued today, or rather he wrote up a report detailing the criminal behavior… and perhaps have a warrant issued by the district attorney. I chose the latter, although I doubted the district attorney would give a hoot about a destroyed table.

I asked the cop to speak to Richard, the tenant who handed me the flag to ensure that Barry would not accuse me of inciting this kind of behavior by "stealing" his flag.

So... he hadn't paid rent due, trashed the picnic table, pooped on the ground, sexually harassed women, threatened others, ignored camp rules, and he wanted to reopen a missing persons case on a woman who had dipped.

To top that off, he was accusing people of stealing the flag he dumped in his fire pit.

This was truly gaslighting. I must defend myself from a madman who made up stories. Why even listen to him?

How about we ignore Barry's paranoia instead? I mean, seriously, I needed to alibi my whereabouts when the flag was "stolen," when it was merely retrieved by a veteran who was furious at the disrespect shown.

I told the sheriff the eviction was served; he grinned and said, "You know we're gonna have to get him out."

I agreed, because I knew Barry was not leaving without a fight. It was now day thirty-three of the eviction notice, and no rent had been paid. There were two days remaining before the lawyer got involved, meaning more paperwork filed with the court showing he'd disregarded the eviction.

Think he'd leave voluntarily? He could have already. Both his RV and vehicle had been repaired for free. Any time he could just hook up and roll out.

And yet, not only was he still here, but he provided a day of chaos on a nice, sunny Sunday.

A little later, he went into the office area. I timed him from the interior of my house as he opened and read his mail. He then peeked over at the camp host to see her reaction. I was paying attention from the front window of the manager's house because if he went into the men's restroom and started shit finger painting on the walls and toilets, a la other evictees, it would be *me* on poop patrol.

He waddled into the restroom, and he was in there for 16 minutes, which was decent, not scary. He then went to his car and messed around some more—slamming the trunk a couple times, the side doors, okay guy, I can hear you.

After he drove off, I checked the restroom, gloved, masked, and goggled. It looked fine, great! It was wonderful!

I was almost slavishly grateful I didn't have to scrape poop off tile and painted walls. Thank you! Thank you! Thank you for not being a dick for a hot minute!

Was I so conditioned that when a freaking abuser doesn't do something awful that I'm grateful? What a pitiful realization.

Because this was a relationship in a messed-up sort of way. I had to think about him and what he was doing. I had to be hyper aware of his behavior for my own protection, and I needed to anticipate his mood, his emotions because if he was restless, or mad…

…. And there was absolutely nothing in it for me.

Crap, I *was* in a relationship.

I so badly wanted to break up with him.

It was Tuesday, and I was doing chores when a couple came up and notified me that Barry's dog was loose again and tried to bite the male tenant. I told him to call the non-emergency hotline to report it and to call animal control as well.

It wasn't the neglected dog's fault. I hoped animal control would confiscate the dog for its own sake and adopt it out to someone who cared.

Lucy, the 18-year-old girl south of Barry, told me that he banged on her mom's trailer (her mom was out of town and most likely would kill Barry when she returned) and he waited outside the door until she opened it.

Then it took a hyper delusional pivot. Barry told Lucy her friend called him and told him everything about his missing flag. Now he demanded to hear it from her.

What? What? WHAT?

Oh, my god. He absolutely knew what happened to his flag. What was wrong with this old asshat harassing a child? Everything he said was a lie! Why was he engaging with her?

I told her to call the non-emergency hotline and report this behavior. And then I gave her pepper spray and showed her how to use it.

Tuesday, the last day on the eviction notice arrived. I called the lawyer and said to get rolling.

One way or the other, he would be out. It would just take a little longer, and the sheriff would be involved.

Wednesday rolled around and the cops were called again by me and then by the camp host.

I was getting ready to leave for a pajama party with pals. The wine and s'mores makings were packed. Barry, in clear violation of the stalking restraining order, marched over to me, Mary, and Sam at the office seating area. He was about four feet away and rapidly muttered disconnected sentences. He smelled so bad, just rank and foul. He was told numerous times by all three of us to go away, he wouldn't, and cops were called.

I went back to my house and waited. Barry was still haranguing Mary and Sam; it was hard to follow his words all tangled together and stampeding at high volume out of his mouth.

I wasn't going out there. I was scared.

Two officers pulled up, exited their truck, and shouted at Barry to back up or he'd be handcuffed. Not once did he stop talking. The words were just a streaming jumble of nonsense, and it was like he couldn't stop. I don't think he had the power to stop.

The hairs on my neck and arms rose. It was a frightening sight to behold.

Even the cops shared a look, like, seriously? They had all been introduced to him several times, but this was on a new level.

I stepped out onto the porch and handed the officer the permanent restraining order, and he called the District Attorney. The other officer was with Barry near the office, just keeping him occupied. This meant Barry was babbling and gesticulating while the officer, who was leaning against sheriff's truck, simply nodded.

The officer asked to come into the house. It seemed that the stalking restraining order had a fatal flaw.

Damned if you do.

Since I didn't want him to shit on the ground in his RV, and needed him use the bathroom, which was between the office and the house, a defense attorney could argue that he was just going to the bathroom (notwithstanding that just moments before he was in the sitting area shouting at everybody and was within four feet from me; thus, violating the order).

"Is it really worthless?" I asked.

He said he wanted to arrest him but knew what the outcome would be. I understood it was stupid to start this process only to have the case dismissed. He said if the bathroom wasn't on the restraining order, he'd have him cuffed in the back of his vehicle.

Damned if you don't.

Late afternoon on Wednesday, I left the campground to play with pals when I got a text from the camp host at about 8:30 p.m. Barry was throwing boots at Lucy's bedroom window to get her attention. Lucy came out and said she would spray him with pepper spray unless he stopped. Again, I told the camp host to tell her to call 911.

Lucy was 18 years old. Barry was hitting an ugly 60 and looked like a blob of cholesterol held together with body odor and long unwashed flesh. How dare he harass a child.

I got home Thursday in the morning from a superb pajama party, unpacked, and started chores. Lee, Lucy's mother, came to the office to speak with me. She said he had damaged her RV slide out by pulling on it. He denied damaging it, but admitted to her that, "I've been throwing little rocks at it."

Lee was very angry and with good reason. I told her to call 911 and to report him for criminal mischief. She said she would.

I then learned from Lee that he had started a fire in the fire pit, which unfortunately, was right under her slide out (a slide out is the unit that literally slides out and makes the interior of the RV larger). That slide out was Lucy's bedroom. He could have shifted the fire pit safely away from her unit, but that was not the point of the fire he was starting.

This was not a fun, "bring out the s'mores fire." This was one that was built to hurt people. It was a dumpster fire.

It was obvious why he started the fire; she cussed him out every which way, and since he couldn't hit her, he was gonna burn her RV.

Lee took off back to her site, and I knew he was not going to stop since his hatred was boundless. I grabbed my fire extinguisher and drove up to his site. Of course, he was getting ready to throw my Astro turf carpet in the growing fire along with a ton of debris he had pulled from the interior of his RV. When I mean pulled from the RV, there was fake wood paneling yanked from the walls of his RV and tilted precariously atop other garbage.

The reek of hot chemicals polluted the air. The fire was smoldering, the smoke was black, oily, and toxic. The smoke looked like a lethal asthma attack. A woman directly across from him had severe respiratory disease and was on oxygen. This would kill her.

Without any fanfare, I parked, Barry screaming at me from his front steps, and grabbed the fire extinguisher, unlocked it by pulling the tab, and walked over to the fire pit. The fire extinguisher did its job in under five seconds. That was fun!

My work here was done.

The plumes of white exhaust scared him, and he backed into his RV, wild eyes wilder. For one minute I was tempted, my finger on the canister's trigger, but no.

He shouted stridently, with a little quaver of adrenaline, "I am allowed to have a fire."

I was not going to argue with him; I was not going to engage.

A campfire in the fire ring should be made of burnable firewood. He started a toxic fire designed to send someone to the ER.

On my way out, I told him, "You also owe me for that burnt Astro turf carpet."

He mumbled, "I don't owe you anything."

The doorbell ding donged again (it was like the 10th time), and Mary said that the sheriff and the fire department were here. I was not going down there. If they had any questions, they could come find me.

What questions? That I put out a fire that would have taken out an innocent woman's RV? I thanked Mary and went back inside. Ding-dong. Mary thought he got put in the back of the Sheriff's truck. I'd check the jail inmate roster when I had a sec. I needed to feed the chickens and the goats. What a day… and it was only 3:30 p.m. It felt like a lot later though. And no, sadly, he wasn't in jail.

A tenant with disabilities was walking her service dog about an hour after the fire extinguisher event. She was across and down the way from Barry, and I spoke to her. She said she hadn't been sleeping more than a few hours, and everyone was on edge because of Barry.

I apologized.

It was now 5:36 p.m.—two hours after conversing with her, the paramedics were at their site.

She wasn't taken to the ER; it was her daughter who suffered from anxiety and a panic attack came on suddenly. Her mom said she'd be okay; it was just the continuing stress of having Barry unpredictably trespass into their site to talk monkey at all hours. Barry watched their site all day and would walk over and bang on their door at random times. To say they were traumatized was an understatement.

Friday, 9/10/21: The attorney came home from vacation, so he should be checking his email shortly; I spoke to his office, so they knew the situation.

I was waiting for a tornado of chaos, which was becoming the norm, but the day was peaceful. The goats got to recess in the dog park, and the chickens enjoyed their corn on the cob.

It rained in the morning but was sunny by midafternoon which saved me the chore of watering. I completed all the testing in the waste treatment plant, chatted up people, and gathered apples for the goats. There are fruit trees at most sites, and wished more people took advantage of them.

The septic truck came to pump out two septic tanks for a total of 5,000 gallons.

I was still on edge and waiting for disaster, but truly, I couldn't ask for a more perfect day.

Saturday: He was still here, and he was in trouble again. There were no cops so far, but he let his dog out and there was a husky next door on a leash, so they got in a fight.

Also, a lumberjack tenant that looked like the lucky charms leprechaun, said that when he went to work around three in the morning Barry, in his RV doorway, was staring at him. I told lucky charms that the dude never sleeps and if he gets concerned, call 911.

One of the tenants alerted me that Barry was under his RV, working on the plumbing. That is simply disgusting since none of the sewage has been removed from underneath his unit.

Barry had already been told that he was not allowed to hook up anything resembling permanent plumbing to my septic system, and yet, there he was.

I went up to his site, hunkered down, and stared at his obese form tightly wedged under there. One, he now had basted himself with his own crap, and two, it didn't look like he knew what he was doing. I straightened and stretched and really wanted to give his magnificent cankles a good kick or two.

"You are not allowed to hook up any permanent plumbing to my septic system," I said as I walked away. He mumbled, "But she's coming back!" No, she's not.

It was 9/11, and he was supposed to be out on 9/7. I racked up the expenses he was going to owe under the rental agreement and decided not to mention it to him. I won't take him to court. Just be gone Barry, just be gone.

I was pushing the mower back to the garage and saw Barry pestering the tenants in another site. I crossed the road and yelled at him get out. He muttered some nonsense about Malice stealing from him, but wait she was coming back, and he fixed the pipes! Why was he in their site babbling about Malice?

I backed him up with pepper spray in hand. The tenants shut the door and I heard the lock click. I moved him toward his site, shouting, "Back up! Nobody likes you! Get out!"

He retreated, but he'd be back; he wouldn't accept that no one wanted contact with him. It was making him manic.

The sheriff came to serve the second round of eviction papers and it was a joyous chorus of texts pinging on my RV park cell.

Did you see?

He's been served!

Yay, Barry was served!

It was like everyone just saw Santa!

Thursday, 9/16/21, the day started out perfectly. The sun was shining, the air was crisp, and the aspens were shaking off their foliage. I did my chores, got the goats out foraging then to the dog park, stopped by at the farm store for supplies to be delivered, and went back to the campground.

And then it began…

I got a text from a tenant. She told Barry to get out of Brenda's site (which was next to his). The tenant said Barry had his junk on Brenda's picnic table. Okay. I drove up, masked and gloved and took the trinket crap from Brenda's table and walked over to his site. I dropped the stuff on his table and yelled at the open RV door. "You leave your junk in another site, [and] it's going in the dumpster next time."

He came out and started mouthing off about how I needed a good fuck, *blah, blah, blah*. Like I haven't heard *that* before.

I got back in my car, and he started screaming, "Where's my flag? Where's my flag? WHERE'S MY FLAG!"

I rolled down the window and shouted gleefully, "I BURNED IT!!!!" We were having a conversation!

I laughed heartily. I could speak fluent crazy. He was still screaming sexually charged insults. I brought my right hand near my face and made a quacking motion with my fingers. That set him off, and I started laughing harder because he looked INSANE.

I never even considered how I looked though…

I drove back to the manager's house, still huffing laughter, and parked the car. Next thing I knew, he'd let his dog loose, again. There was this revenge reaction every time I called him out on some dick move.

Lee texted me that she was calling the cops about the dog. Then she texted back and said she was calling 911 again because he now repeatedly slammed a piece of lumber against her RV.

What I found out was that Jay—a nice guy, had a good dog— came out of his RV to confront Barry as he spun and banged the lumber against Lee's RV.

Barry then turned on him in an instant and began approaching Jay with such malevolence, that Jose, a tenant two doors down from this drama, was concerned enough to step outside, knife in hand, and confronted Barry, who was too close to Jay. Once he saw the knife, Barry backed up, still holding the plank of wood.

I started back up the lane and saw Jose and Jay. There was no knife in sight at that time (I learned about the above mayhem when I walked up), and there was a ton of noise coming from Barry's.

All this commotion woke Cheryl, who worked nights, and she was outside her RV.

I walked by her and said, "Call 911, this guy is out of control, site 21, they'll know."

What I didn't know until later, and why three officers appeared so quickly, was that Jay had called 911 and told them that unless they got "that guy" off the property, he was going to kill him… on a *recorded* 911 call. Jesus.

And because there were numerous separate 911 calls within a matter of minutes…

After getting caught up on current events with the tenants, I went back down to the office and spoke with a potential tenant. He got an application and I showed him the available site, and then walked him back to the office. It was there that I came upon two officers while a third one drove up to Barry and the people who had called. I assured the potential tenant that no, this was not normal, but we had a guy getting evicted and he was going off the rails.

One of the cops said, "Don't turn around, don't move, just keep looking at me." From the corner of my eye, I could see a slow-moving flash of white and stayed perfectly still. This was a weird game we were playing. Even the prospective tenant beside me didn't move.

"Okay," the cop grinned, "He's off the property. Now if he tries to come back, we'll arrest him for trespass." I turned and saw the rear of the RV flash brake lights as it turned south down the highway. Barry had become such a daily mental onslaught that I couldn't belief he just… left.

My relief was palpable as the other cop said he was going to call the other officers and let them know it was over. I thanked them for their service, and one cop said that he and the others, as soon as their shift ended, were going for beers.

What a great day! People commented that the air felt different, and the tension was gone. That infernal malevolent maelstrom had left the property.

We had created a community for the most part and looked out for each other. That same community banded together and made him leave. The first time he attempted to pull out the RV, the jacks were down, and he was shouting and fussing with that when the officer rolled up. He finally got them retracted and drove out, but the real impetus were all the people upset with his behavior. Everything came to a head that afternoon and I was glad Barry made the decision to leave before things got worse. For him.

I imagined it must have terrified Barry to see tenants coming at him and forcing him to leave. I thought the cop may have also had a word with him. It was enough to get him gone, finally. Thank God.

I enjoyed Jose's comment that since Jay confessed on that 911 call, we could have all participated in a murder and just blamed Jay.

Yes, a community of which I'm proud to be a part.

Oh, and that potential tenant? He didn't come back.

I spent an hour using disinfectant on the area, including that RV black water waste tank filled with congealed poop and toilet paper. What a parting gift.

I told everyone to stay away and let the chlorine do its job. I would take the gravel and the plastic sheeting covered in feces and chlorine to the dumpsters tomorrow since they would be emptied in the morning. I was not going to try to dump crap in the full dumpster today and have chlorine and poop drip out.

Bon voyage Barry.

I don't believe Barry had long to live; his right leg, from ankle to knee, was a curious purple color. It looked like raw liver encased in a pulsating sheath of hot damp skin the color of tapioca, but it was translucent, swollen to the point of bursting. I figured it was an infection from his banging around tearing apart the RV's interior or maybe cutting himself on the broken picnic table, or paneling, or glass shards from his father's military shadow box.

Or maybe when he was shitting in his RV, some of that e-coli and coliforms dripped into an open wound. That stuff will kill you.

He didn't have enough sense to realize he was chock full of sepsis as that infection crept up his leg. Lunacy doesn't need no stinking wellness check.

It looked like a cellulitis kielbasa.

Cellulitis Kielbasa: playing at Coachella and opening for My Chemical Romance.

Lee, in the site south of now vacant 21, asked me if the next person in that site could be a nice, single gentleman. Someone between the ages of 50 and 70, attractive, but can have a walker, if necessary.

I told her Ted Bundy had reserved the site. She laughed and said at least *he* was attractive.

As I walked back toward the house, pulled off my plastic gloves and dropped them in the dumpster, I heard the cell phone in my back pocket ping.

In the house after my hands were thoroughly washed, I read a text from Maris who lived next door to a woman named Bunny. Goddamn it. I just got off unchecked mental illness island with Barry, did the boat turn around and go back?

We will talk about Bunny after T-Rexes and lonely people. I can't segue into a story about another unstable tenant just yet. I need a break. I'm sure you do too.

PALATE CLEANSER

An unusual winter storm

T-REX

As one would expect, T-Rexes have very short arms, and thus, can't do much for themselves.

One of the many T-Rexes who resided at the campground and are predominantly male, called twice and left me messages that the shower curtain in the men's restroom was on the floor. Two messages.

The shower curtain is a standard tension rod put between two walls until it's tight. There are two separate rods with two plastic shower curtains—one white for the inner side, which is the one that fell, and the other one, pretty on the outside, which was allegedly still up.

I guess T-Rex couldn't reach with such short arms. Did I really have to explain to you, dear reader, how a shower curtain works? He waited outside the bathroom door, pacing and T-Rex could see I was in the meadow shearing a cashmere goat.

For once I didn't say mowing. Well, that's a different kind of mowing, I suppose.

I went back to work on Oreo and got her pretty. The cashmere wool went in the dumpster; I'd waited too long, and it was too matted to salvage.

T-Rex had gone back to his site by the time I hung up the shower curtain. I know he didn't work here, but really?

Sigh.

I called him and left a message, sharing the good news that it was now in its rightful place.

He called back to let me know that now he could take a shower. He did say thank you, but damn.

Sigh.

Another T-Rex walked over to tell me the garden hose was on in the meadow. He was out there, Paul Blartted the situation, and reported it to me. He didn't turn it off while he was out there.

Seriously?

One T-Rex ding-donged and asked earnestly, if Amazon delivered on Sunday. I looked over at the empty area where Amazon deliveries were stored, then back to him, and asked, "Did you check your tracking?"

He stared at me, then shook his head. I shrugged and went back inside because I do not deliver for Amazon. I thought, *was this necessary on a quiet Sunday while I was trying to eat a late lunch? Hmmm? I mean, seriously, was this convo critical? You waiting on insulin? No? Didn't think so.*

One of the T-Rexes stopped asking me for help because I stopped helping. Oh, at first, I was willing. But soon I realized that this would lead to a pattern of behavior.

No, I can't go into your RV to program your TV.

No, I cannot help you dump your black and gray tanks.

No, I checked the mailbox a half an hour ago. You haven't had any mail since a half an hour ago when you asked.

No, I cannot do all the chores you should, as a grown ass adult, be able to do by yourself.

T-Rexes lived alone and were lonely. If they were married, they were simply called husbands and the wife could take care of everything. She would be a T-Rex wrangler.

I get that family is far away, but please don't manufacture problems so that we have something to talk about.

There was a Ford F-150 truck on the property which was about two sites up from one T-Rex, and said truck was parked adjacent to the meadow, not anywhere near his site— keep that in mind.

It had become his mission (the truck had been there for at least a year. The owners moved out six months ago) to ask me, every day, when the truck would be moved off the property.

It made me cringe. My neck muscles, those along the tops of the shoulders, would tighten up and crawl toward my ears *every time* I saw him because he would ask, "So what about that truck?"

He didn't have a vehicle, the truck was not near his site, and even though it wasn't impinging on his lifestyle in any manner, it had certainly caught his eye.

What about it? Even if I towed it off the property, he would find something else to talk about, like the roosters that enjoyed yelling at his windows at 6:00 a.m. This is true; they come over to my bedroom window and start catcalling at dawn.

They were supposed to be Rhode Island Red hens, not roosters. I know, I know. What did he want me to do? Wring their necks? They are such pretty boys.

One of the T-Rexes complained that a tenant told him to "fuck off" after he insisted she not pet his dog that he had on leash within a foot of her. What did he expect? T-Rex had his friendly dog almost in her lap.

And why was he telling me? What a tattletale.

Unlike the movies, if you stop moving, a T-Rex can still see you. T-Rexes approached while I sorted the mail, at the computer in the office, herding the goats or mowing the lawn; T-Rexes attacked at any time.

One T-Rex related that he was the middle child, and his birthday was coming up. One of the tenants (a talented artist), had crocheted this T-Rex a matching scarf and beret as a birthday present. T-Rex rocked the Where's Waldo-ish look in that getup, but I kept that to myself as he was telling me about the dog he had when he was eight years old who was best friends with his cat and can I check the mail again right now because it's important to him and his lawn needs mowing right now.

Or could he let his dog loose in the meadow to play catch with a frisbee? Or could he have a box of dog poop bags for his very own, or, or… hold on, someone's ding donging at the office.

Just got back in the house, and it had been pouring rain. There was some sort of cyclone bomb storm that had dropped six plus inches in ten days.

I had to go up to a T-Rex's site, he said his electricity was out. I asked him if he checked the breakers in his RV. He answered, "Yes, [it] doesn't work." I asked if he checked the breakers at the pedestal. He said, "Yes, it's not working. The electricity is out."

Really?

Nope, the electricity was not out. I know, because I took my desk lamp up there, shielded it from the torrential downfall with my overly large windbreaker picked up at Goodwill, and plugged it into the outlet on the pedestal from which all electricity was derived, and *presto*! Let there be light.

I could be back at my house. I needed to poop.

The lamp shone brightly in the early November gloom, making the rain sparkle in the downpour. It was beautiful.

I looked at him and shrugged. I really didn't want to get mad because it was not good for me. He then went inside for a minute, came back out, and told me that he fixed the breakers, and that the electricity was working. Now.

He said this proudly, with no apology or irony involved.

As I stood with my shining living room lamp (which now had a wet lampshade) I wondered, T-Rex, why didn't you check the breakers before running down to ding dong me with a pretend problem?

Did you need me to cut your meat too? Any other things I could do for you when I could be home and dry?

Christmas evening, December 25, 2021: It was snowing. At 9:20 p.m. I was enjoying a quiet moment with an edible and four cabin fevered felines (one of which wasn't mine but had decided to stay for an extended pajama party. She was no idiot; it was below freezing outside). There was a lot of hissing, purring, and jockeying for position on the comforter. Merry Christmas to all, and to all...

Ding dong, ding dong! What? I got up, went to the front door and saw a T-Rex standing at the bottom of the ramp. He was a little drunk. I knew he spent Christmas day down south at a casino with a friend, and they do overserve, so he was entitled and moderately outraged that he had no electricity in his RV and it was snowing.

Okay, was this going to be a repeat of the night it rained like a mother? I asked him that, and he said he had checked ALL the breakers. I asked if they were tripped, and he said no. Okay, I went inside and got my hat, coats, rubber boots on, and that reading lamp from the desk and carefully navigated the snow on the ramp. The last thing I needed was to break my ass.

Tromping up the snow-covered road, my $24.00 rubber boots made that skritch, skritch, corn starchy noise. I got to his site, plugged in the lamp and *viola*, let there be light, again. I just stared at him for a minute, trying not to lose my shit. This was a rerun. I told him *again*, as I showed him how to turn the breakers at the pedestal off and on. The lamp was turning off and on, so the problem was inside the RV, and it had nothing to do with my electrical.

The snow was falling silently and delicately; it looked beautiful in the gold glow of the lamp. So fragile, lacy, pretty and mesmerizing but damn, my face was freezing.

So again, nothing was wrong with the electrical pedestal. Something was going on inside his RV.

I unplugged my lamp with chilled fingers and told him to get in that RV and see if the breakers had been tripped. I said he could not continue to plug in his toaster, microwave, *and* heater to the same plug.

I was not going into this man's RV, that was not going to happen. I've seen that movie.

I retreated to my house to get back into bed with the remainder of my relaxed vibes and the Travel Channel.

But wait, there was more! Sunday after Christmas, he was back ding donging saying he had very little electrical outlets working in his RV.

Again, I asked, "Did you check the breakers?" And again, he swore he did. He said he was cold, and I asked, "What do you want me to do about it? I'll call my electrician to check out the pedestal on Monday to make sure that's not the problem, but I'm pretty sure it's not since there's no tripping and the power is there."

He complained again that he was freezing, and I just looked at him, like, what? What? He said he'd called the RV repair guy, but he couldn't come out until Tuesday or Wednesday. I didn't know where he was going with this. He kept saying he was cold. T-Rex, you are not my kid.

He then asked for the lamp that I brought out yesterday, stating that his lights weren't working in his RV. I gave it to him and wondered why he wanted that light since he didn't have power, but if it got him gone, I didn't care.

Once inside, I confirmed with the electrician that he'd be here tomorrow, Monday, 12/27/21 to check out the pedestal even though I was positive it was working. That confirmation would run me about $150.00, just so I could get this freaking T-Rex off my porch. Maybe $150.00 wasn't such a big price to pay for peace and quiet.

Monday follow up: The electrician showed up around dusk. It was a very snowy day. The low was 18 and the high was 30. I'd been running around disconnecting frozen water lines, pouring warm water over the faucets, and starting small trickles so that the water wouldn't freeze and blow out the spigots.

Of course, there was nothing wrong with the electrical pedestal and that was told to T-Rex. Like I said, but I wasn't believed. Now, good sir, you know the electrical issue was inside your house and your problem. The electrician, a guy, explained it to T-Rex in the exact same language I used, but T-Rex was clearly satisfied with the electrician's answer and yet disregarded mine.

He did give me back the lamp he'd borrowed the other day. He didn't say much, except for a story about how he slept for almost 12 hours. I was standing in the falling snow with no mittens, and my ears were burning while he was cozy in his doorway. I replied, "Well, maybe you needed it." Then of course my snotty mind said, *you don't need it; you don't do anything.* Then it followed up with, *just shut up; don't be a dick. You don't know him.*

It's just weird sometimes just how much people share. Now that's an ironic statement. Do I have any self-awareness of what *I've* been doing?

CHATTYSENIORS.COM

Most of my conversations with single older people on site were driven by loneliness, but the T-Rex above was simply lazy idiocy. Why did I have to prove it wasn't my fault (my pedestal), when, if he'd hired an electrician, he could have found out whose fault it was (which was his with a much higher probability.)

Now he still had to hire an electrician. And that tale about sleeping beauty? Maybe he should tighten the reins on his sleeping pills? But why share that personal information with me? Yay, you slept almost a whole day! What did you want from me? A round of applause? A gold star?

If I had to communicate with every tenant, every day, to alleviate their loneliness… Well, there aren't enough hours in the day, and nothing would get accomplished.

Loneliness can't ever be sated; it is such a hungry, ravenous emotion. It's as if contentment had a tapeworm that just kept eating away at the happiness and needed to be fed, fed, fed.

I'm sorry folks, sometimes it just becomes a bit much for me.

Please don't come out while I'm mowing because you want me to turn off the mower and pay attention to you when there's absolutely nothing of import you want to relay.

Stop watching me mow; it's creeping me out. Don't tell me I looked tired yesterday, after mowing two acres, I was.

Did I mention that I'm not a people person? This stuff wears me out; it literally exhausted me. This mental toll of paying attention is even harder than mowing two acres. Too bad empathy doesn't burn any calories.

I've come to relish my four-hour drive to drop off my poop samples at the testing laboratory. Nice and quiet. I would listen to Morbid with the windows rolled up and the doors locked.

I was thinking of a possible business venture to solve my problem with this widespread loneliness. I'm sure it's a byproduct of the pandemic but also because people don't seem to have a rich tapestry of relationships on which to rely.

So, the solution: It's kind of like if Care.com and Match.com fell in love and had a baby that grew up to match older people not on looks or compatibility, except for tales they want to endlessly repeat. Long winded stories, sagas, fireside tales, hunting stories, war stories, fishing stories, long haul trucking stories, happy childhood stories, sad childhood stories, grandchildren stories, stories of their pets, vacations, endless road trips, good meals, and best pets. Oh, and my favorite to date: medical procedures and illnesses. *When did you get that appendix removed, knee replaced, spine surgery? Tell me again!* I don't need to muck out the goat pens, run the waste treatment plant, clean the restrooms, finish this year's continuing education, pay bills, collect rent, or unclog toilets!

It never gets old! Puleease! More stories!

I mean Farmersonly.com is a thing, so why can't chattyseniors. com be a thing? Well, I bought the domain name, just in case.

It's so crazy that it just might work!

The biggest problem with this idea is that many of these older folks are terrified of technology. Since we are going to be cloistered and segregated for months, this might be the new reality. If we get their kids and grandkids, or for heaven's sake, the senior centers to set up FaceTime on tablets and do a tutorial showing how easy it is to join, then we could have seniors telling seniors remarkably similar stories. Can it work? Can it save me 30 plus listening hours a week?

For a nominal fee, one can search the list of like-minded seniors who want to chat about shared interests.

How many kidney stones? Wow, that's a lot!

These aren't seniors looking for love, these are seniors looking for a listener. This could work. They don't want to meet in person or have a physical relationship; they just want to tell their stories. These long-distance relationships are as good as in person with FaceTime, since you know, old people don't like to travel. When they do go out, they want to get back home as soon as possible. It is like they are already planning their escape route from a concert thirty minutes before it's over.

Loneliness has been the biggest issue among so many.

This might work. Instead of a crackhead phone tree, it could be a chatty seniors' phone tree. Then, if somebody was not coming up to their arranged FaceTime call, their friend could request a wellness check from the local authorities. I've fallen and I can't get up, but chattyseniors.com saved my life! Thanks, Edna!

Hmmm...

Maybe not even FaceTime, but just regular phone calls. Let's ditch the technology and have them correspond by mail, and chat on the phone. Let's take a giant leap backward, since this is where all the stories they want to share are coming from anyway.

Hmmm...

Oh, and as a fantastic and rare moment of self-awareness regarding the talky, talky, talky... I apologize to everyone for every time I chit-chatted uber long stories about nothing you're even remotely interested in and it's probably not even the first time you've heard it.

My bad that I yammered on and on about people you don't know and don't care about. My bad and I appreciate that you never yawned or rolled your eyes. Thank you.

Oh, wait. Wait!

UNCHECKED MENTAL ISSUES—CONTINUED

Now, back to your regularly scheduled lunacy: I got a text from Maris regarding Bunny, her next-door neighbor.

The text was sent mere hours after Barry exited the property, and the cops took off for happy hour. I was too tired to deal with this, but I drew the short straw.

Well, I always drew the short straw. After Barry's departure, I started the cleaning process and was tired. The last thing I wanted was another emotional explosion but that's what I got.

This remarkable, over-the-top fearful suspicion Bunny had had graduated into aggressive posturing toward whoever/whomever/whatever she thought was currently victimizing her.

Kind of like a dog that's aggressive because it's scared.

I can't speak to anything that happened off property, but all her contentions of danger she alleged occurred on-site. Well, that's not true; she had told me of being surveilled off property and people listened in on her calls, thus the burner phones and valid no email. Bunny lived in a state of perpetual threat. I cannot imagine the stress of maintaining that level of looking both ways.

Two Notices to Quit highlighted our fractious relationship. I had infiltration into the sewer system on the property and had technicians with cameras and specialized equipment searching to find where the water was entering the system from rainfall and groundwater. Was it the manholes? The main line? The laterals? These guys worked at $425 an hour to find my infiltration, and Bunny just couldn't stop herself from constantly interfering. The workers complained that every time I turned my back to go work on something else, she would creep out of her RV and harass them.

She told the workers that there was a cougar on her roof and that the children were in danger. She said she was poisoned by the water supply and several people here were violently sick. She said her water pressure was dangerous, and it was so high that they needed to come over and do something about it immediately. I've heard all of this before and didn't realize she shared this news.

This happened during the two days that they were here. First day she got a notice. Second day she got a notice because she wouldn't stop. I'm pretty sure if the workers were here a third day, that she would have also gotten a third notice.

Even if I was "poisoning" her somehow with a municipal water supply, these guys were on the clock and knew their job. They had zero to do with the water supply. That should give some insight into her frame of mind…Anyone who would listen to her conspiracy theories was fair game.

Maris was stuck living next to a woman who was seriously paranoid to the point where I worried that her delusions would push her to violence. I believed she had weapons, and I believed she truly had committed to her reality. I didn't know she wasn't living on the property for several months because she would show up, and I guess just check her inventory of crap and then leave. It turned out her RV was completely uninhabitable, a leaking roof, leaking pop outs, no functioning toilet, just a moldy hovel.

Her son had cut off contact because he couldn't deal with her. I had asked him if he knew where she was, if he had a phone number or a valid email address, and if she was going to pay rent. He said he had no idea how to reach her, and in hindsight, I think he meant in any fashion.

I was sure Bunny's actions made sense to her. Bunny had a rich interior life filled with unimaginable dangers.

Maybe it made her feel special, important, a part of something bigger, some weird secret handshake making her one of the people who *knew*. She was the one with the cougar on the roof, no one else. I think she desired to be unique.

Who am I to tell her she's just like the lot of us? She was just a human being working her way to the grave. She was a dead man walking, and the clock was ticking.

I hoped Bunny enjoyed her Cheerios and milk that morning. It might not be her last bowl, but one day, with absolute certainty, there *will be* one last bowl of Cheerios. Sorry.

Geez that got dark.

Back to the text I received from Maris:

Bunny is here with a U-Haul (which I knew, she was moving stuff out of an RV that is uninhabitable) *so I asked if she was getting a new trailer. She went off and now she said the sheriff, the state, the tribal police all know about me. And that you (meaning me the manager) are done with me. I told her to leave me alone and she said, I SEE YOUR DEMON!*

I See Your Demon, playing at KROQ's weenie roast.

Tribal Police? The Forum.

I texted back: *be careful, stay inside until she loads her trailer's contents to the U-Haul.* I almost texted *if you feel threatened, please call 911,* but then I thought about all the Barry shit for the last eight weeks, and now, I was asking for another 911 call. Nope, can't, no. We cannot load the cops with the next crazy in less than five hours. These guys needed a break; last time we talked, they were going for congratulatory beers.

I should have offered to buy a round. They earned it.

Bunny, on her way out of the campground, in the U-Haul—which should be going to the dump, not a storage facility—stopped and said that Maris, her nearest neighbor, drilled into her locks on her RV.

No, she didn't. What did she want me to do about this imaginary crime?

Bunny had to stop, ding dong, and relate this to me on her way to her storage unit on her first round of garbage storage duty.

She was adamant that Maris was the culprit. She believed that Maris, a stranger, drilled into her lock to steal her stuff even though nothing was taken. The locks, all ten plus of them, were securely in place, and Bunny wanted me to know about the felonious activities of Maris...

I don't get headaches, but I felt a twitch coming on under my right eye. Tic, tic, tic, damn. Was it noticeable?

I asked, "Do you really think your neighbor got a drill to break into your place and what? Did she (air quotes) 'steal' anything?"

These are the locks that Maris supposedly picked, and then relocked.

Look at those impressive chains. I should've congratulated Maris on her *Ocean's Eleven* skill. She was able to break in and NOT steal the queen's jewels, all the while leaving the locks locked after the caper was completed.

Bunny ignored my incredulous question and righteously held up a piece of metal—circular and perhaps two inches long, a half an inch wide, and didn't look drilled at all or that belonged to any lock mechanism— and said, "I had to have the locksmith come out today and replace this!"

There had been *no* locksmith on the property that day. I should know because there was only one locksmith in town, and we were familiar. He knew the drill, no pun intended. Every visitor must sign in at the office, and he hadn't. Whatever she was holding was most likely not from a lock.

But the way she was holding it toward the sky made it seem like this was direct proof of the thief next door. It was all so clear now! She had concrete proof that Maris was a thief!

Why was it important to convince me? Why was I being invited to this mad dance when I wasn't dressed for it?

Welcome back to unchecked mental illness island.

She continued, "That woman slyly mentioned stuff I had in my house, so she was in there!"

Slyly? Okay, yeah.

Unless, *unless* she was freaking Bunny out, then running inside and texting me all innocent like… *Oh Christ, it's catching!*

Again, when the guy came to move Bunny's RV, she had to have him use his bolt cutters to cut through her many locks since she didn't have all the keys. Did Maris have all the keys to those locks? Or did she use her talents to unlock, creep in, look around slyly, exit, then relocked them all, save for the one that she drilled through…?

Bunny was convinced that Maris got a drill, drilled into ONE of the locks, and got in her RV. Maris didn't take anything but taunted her with her extensive knowledge of Bunny's inventory. It never occurred to Bunny that none of this made any reasonable sense.

Maris had made it a point to hide in her RV from Bunny, so no conversation ever took place. Should I have brought that up? Should I have continued to argue?

While I was pondering the above, Bunny muttered weird nonsense, hatred, and venom about her neighbor Maris and all the people she distrusted. I didn't clearly hear what she said but I got the general gist of her vitriol—quick chatter, monotone, eyes twitching side to side, looking up, rolling—and she never once looked me in the eyes.

I didn't interrupt this delusional riff; there was no reason to reply. Also, she wasn't really talking to me.

Very alarming. That was not the first time I've seen potentially violent mental illness up close (Barry), but I was chilled, because at that point, there was no reasoning with her. Nothing I said could de-escalate the situation.

She was on a roll… downhill.

Disclaimer: I don't have a degree in psychology; I'm an accountant, okay? But Barry in the morning and Bunny in the afternoon was just entirely too much.

Before Bunny took a running leap completely over the paranoia cliff, she held it together for several years and managed to work, pay rent, and keep her site together. Over time, more locks were added, more chains were extended, and more crap was left outside.

She was, without a doubt, certain in her beliefs about people tracking her. She believed she had relatives in law enforcement who told her that. She also believed that she was from gypsy blood and could see the future.

Frankly, I don't think "gypsies" go around talking about their "gypsy blood." Besides, aren't they Roma? Just asking, but I'm pretty sure that "gypsy" is pejorative.

She once called me and said that she was concerned about the way some of the men at the park talked about me, and she said I should have a weapon of some type.

That was disconcerting, so I went down to the hunting and fishing supply store and looked at tasers. I should have thought that through; I'm not a worrier, and she could have just been projecting her fears regarding single women out in her utterly scary world, but what the hell.

At that time, there were about three sketchy guys on the property, and one of whom I had to repeatedly tell to back off my porch and meet me at the office. He's dead now, so no worries. He died on the toilet, as his cousin relayed the death facts to me. Don't know why I needed to know that, or why you did as well… It was off property at the cousin's house, so there was no ghost running around here with its pants down.

I did not want a firearm, not with my temper, and tasers are non-lethal. The sales guy walked me through it, and I said, "I think this is the wrong battery; it should be a D battery not a 9 volt." He pulled out a D battery and inserted it into the taser, and from there it went downhill.

He'd inadvertently turned it on, tased himself, brushed up on me while he was jumping around and man that was a powerful current.

During his impressive solo tango that took down the Christmas decorations behind him, I heard giggling from the girl standing next to me. Then I started laughing as the guy shakily stood up from behind the counter. The little girl and I rehung the tinsel on the counter that had gotten pulled off while I told the dazed, tased sales guy, "I'll take it."

I haven't used it, and hopefully never will.

Bunny had this unfounded paranoia that everybody was out to get her, and I mean *everybody*. She usually picked a target and focused that laser suspicion on that person—no evidence, no reasonable allegations, just full-bore hatred and vehemence.

It was both a global conspiracy and a narrow-eyed speculation on her newest singular target.

This paranoia didn't last for long on any individual since she was an equal opportunity hater. For a while, it was me who was her mortal enemy.

She accused me of poisoning her drinking water. I told her it came from a municipal water agency, and I had nothing to do with it.

She said the water pressure was so high it was shooting out of her faucets and damaging her system. I got a pressure gauge and showed her it was normal.

That brief hatred toward me eventually passed. I guess she couldn't figure out anything else that could be my fault and would which put her in immediate peril.

She said homeless people were skulking about in the middle of the night and looking in her windows. I asked her twenty plus immediate neighbors and they saw nothing. There was a bulldog directly across the lane, and that animal would have called out an alarm if he saw anything.

Bunny repeatedly said at night there was a cougar that sat on her RV's roof. If there *was* a cougar, then there wouldn't be any gangs of chickens roaming about. However, if I had brought that up, she would have made some excuse, like the chickens flew away and escaped.

There was nothing I could do to prove something doesn't exist. I couldn't prove a negative.

"If there was a cougar on top of your RV, what did you want me to do about that?" I had asked her.

It was a stupid question, and that was my bad. She said, "I want the kids to wear bells and bang pots together to scare them away when they are outside playing."

Okay, so you want to turn the kids into dinner bells? Capital idea!

(I told this to the camp host. She said, "Noisier kids? I'll kill the kids before the cougar does.")

Some people like drama. Maris next door could have been her friend. Instead, Bunny went out of her way to pick fights and cause conflict.

Does internal chaos interfere with introspection? Yessir. Does external conflict and antagonism suppress the riot of internal chaos? Most likely.

I answered the office doorbell, and there was an older fellow waiting to move Bunny's mold encrusted trailer out of the site and install another one in its place. I gave him my number and asked him for his to give to Bunny. Bunny didn't have anything but a burner phone, you know, for those shady people who also tracked her through chemtrails, not contrails.

The guy, Bob, said that Bunny didn't want to empty out her RV here because her next-door neighbor (Maris) was looking at her stuff like she was going to steal it. He said he was to take the entire mess to his property so she could empty it out there. After, he would then bring the other RV trailer back to install.

He said he'd come back in an hour and see if Bunny was there.

After that interruption, I was just starting to fall asleep for an afternoon nap. It was rainy and cold and quiet for a hot minute and my textbook was on my lap, open. I was mentally and physically exhausted,

Dingdong again, and it was Bunny. She was back with the U-Haul. I told her to call Bob because he was here in town because of the arrangement to move it out and install a new one.

It pissed me off that nobody could contact her so neither I nor the trailer guy could reach her.

She said, "Oh, I changed my mind about that RV, and you need photos of a RV to approve, correct?"

I nodded. "Here's Bob's number. Please call him, he's waiting on you."

Let her explain to the gentlemen why she was no longer agreed to their deal. I didn't want to be between those two or that transaction.

I am not your concierge, and now don't go T-Rexing on me.

Bunny then asked if site 21 was open. That caught me by surprise. OMG, did she really think I was going to put a different kind of crazy in there? Also, Barry just left, and it was still filthy; I would remove the poop tank the next day, and finish the disinfection, just too beat from all the shenanigans to continue the cleanup.

Barry also screwed with the tiny white Christmas lights plugged in the site to illuminate the cherry tree in the next site. Why be such a dick? And Barry, just a hint, putting magnets all over the 30- and 50-amp outlets doesn't do squat, but nice try.

Move Bunny where Barry just vacated? Her paranoia was disturbing, but I had her in the last site in the back so her north and west sides were pasture and forest. There were no neighbors to accuse of spying and stealing and then there was poor Maris to the south.

She couldn't be in a more populated area because she would be suspiciously watching them all, thinking they were watching her, when they didn't even give a shit. And it was a racket when she started to unlock her RV.

Yes, that is a brass cowbell. Can always use more cowbell.

And all that stuff outside the RV? Who knows? She didn't have children for the kiddie pool, and she didn't use a walker. Go figure.

She was not built for a pleasant, sane, society. And I couldn't do this to our community.

Move Bunny? Hold up. She owed rent for September, and she was moving out the mold filled one and didn't have another. Did she think I was just going to hold it open with no money? I had a waiting list. I told you she was delusional. I had gotten so engrossed in the moving out antics that I'd forgotten about the back rent.

I told her that that site was taken.

After she left, I walked back to look at her site, and there were tire marks UP the raised sewer riser… seriously?

Good god, the movers were on the sewer riser that I just repaired. They were gone now, and I would need to open it up to see if they crushed the plastic septic riser. They would be back to move her RV. I moved an orange cone that was over the pumping system to that area, just to stay off an obvious sewer structure.

Back in the house, I lay down on the sofa and put my homework back in my lap. Just for a minute folks, please. Please, I was so tired.

Nope. The cell phone pinged. Texts were coming in.

Maris was giving me text updates on the pile of crap Bunny was leaving outside the RV.

Bunny was ding donging at the office to propel me out of the house and from reading Maris' texts. She told me that Maris cut back the blackberries. How dare she cut back her first line of defense against the invading hordes coming to steal her treasures?

There were four cows and their babies in the field next door. They were Bunny's nearest neighbors besides Maris.

That nap was now just a fond memory. What was I thinking? A quiet couple of hours on a late, drizzly afternoon?

I watched Bunny exit the property; she'd be back tomorrow for more fun and games.

I went to bed early for an exhausted dreamless sleep.

The next day, Maris texted that Bunny (the second day of U-hauling, transferred disgusting, damaged, and moldy belongings into a U-Haul in order to store them somewhere else) was saying and doing some crazy shit, which included backing the U-Haul into the picnic table and benches. What was up with people trashing my picnic tables and benches?

Bunny poured liquid out of gallon plastic milk containers onto the gravel/grass site and was making sure nobody watched her. But somebody was, her arch nemesis Maris.

Maris later told me it was urine in those jugs. She had a black light and shined it over the area.

Just unpack that sentence. Somebody had a black light to look at bodily fluids. Wait, somebody had stored urine in numerous milk jugs?

I developed a tic in my right eye.

The idea of a tenant pouring urine from plastic milk jugs onto the ground because her toilet hadn't worked for months, and she hadn't been living there for months, and yet there were plastic milk jugs she was pouring onto the ground now... I can't even.

Christ on a crutch, really?

And then my pragmatic brain started to figure out how one would have to pee in a larger container first, maybe a pot for cooking pasta, then use a funnel to pour it into an empty milk jug because no one has that accurate an aim and, why, why why? Why pour it out now? Just cap that plastic milk container and put that stuff into the dumpster, not onto the ground!

But wait, Maris had a black light and went over and Nancy Drew'd what Bunny had poured out, ugh, what is going on? Why do I need to know this?

Maris told me via text that Bunny was throwing more crap out of the RV onto the lawn instead of carrying it to the U-Haul.

It had rained three inches in 48 hours. What was Bunny thinking? Wait, it turned out she wasn't because Maris texted that Bunny was outside Maris' RV, serenading her. Maris texted:

.....She sang me a stalker song. I will save in my laptop. She sang Maris is from another planet.......She is NUTS says she will never leave here. All that I had sung to my RV! Was she like this before?

I texted that she had gotten worse over the past few months, and she was looking to pick a fight.

I also let Maris know that she could file a restraining order against her, which could read no communication, no threatening singing, and no contact. They were free to file in the county, and maybe that would help because calling 911 to report threatening behavior (please refer to Barry) didn't help unless they had something to work with, like a restraining order.

Maris texted that she thought there was some weird power struggle going on between them that she didn't even know about. I texted, *it could be anyone near her,* you're just collateral damage. (I didn't text that last part about collateral damage.)

I should have evicted Bunny when the eviction moratorium ended, and one could evict without cause on anyone renting for less than a year.

It was my own fault I missed that deadline. She came by to pay rent for the lopsided trailer held together by locks and black mold. I got greedy and got paid by the invisible tenant who only occasionally came by to harass Maris or pasted poster boards offering Tarot card readings, $5 donations, or advertised random garage sales of her stuff, where nothing was ever sold and got jammed back into the RV at the end of the day.

The mover returned. What looked to be a short gig for the mover guy turned into the Bataan Death March.

I was talking to the middle-aged gentleman mover at Bunny's site when Bunny rolled up. The first thing out of her mouth was, "Who are you? Please show me your identification!"

He pulled out his wallet and told her he was the guy working for the guy she hired. She rudely grabbed at the driver's license, nodded after looking at it, and handed it back.

Even though he was still a total stranger to her, that production of a legal document made her, weirdly, even more aggressive. "You were supposed to be here at 1:00 p.m." Her face was colored with anger, and she directed her ire at this guy who was just trying to move her RV.

I lost my temper and said, "It's 12:55 p.m. Bunny, what is the issue? He's early by five minutes!"

That took the wind out of her sails, and she explained to me, in tedious detail, that her car's clock must be too fast, or too slow, or planning something against her, and that poor man was now tethered to her until he could get it hooked up and off the property and get her gone.

I left, not interested in tickets to that circus. That poor guy… he had no idea that morning that he was going to waste time on this adventure.

It took hours, from cutting through all the locks (should have asked Maris to lock pick all of them again) to her being indecisive on what to keep or throw away. All the while he was just standing there, waiting for her to get out of the way so he could put up the jacks and unhook the hookups. Good god, all this was done in the pouring rain.

Finally, it was all hooked up and moved out.

Before she followed him to wherever, she stopped and dingdonged at the office, which rang in the house. I came out to stand on the covered porch, and it was still raining.

Bunny came to me and stood in the pouring rain. She said she would be installing a RV on the property. I countered with, "The rent must be paid in full before the 5th. I've let you slide for months paying partial payments, [but] that's done, and I have veto power over what you bring on the property."

Her response? "Are these terms that everybody has to adhere to?"

"You mean pay rent on time and have a suitable RV? Yes."

She said she'd "get back" to me.

So, she had about a week to pay rent.

I was getting more nervous the closer that date came. There were no calls from Bunny, no messages, and no appearances whatsoever.

I didn't want her to come back onto the property; I didn't want the headache of her harassing Maris and focusing all her hatred on a stranger.

No Bunny on the fifth. I breathed a sigh of relief and called the woman who wanted that site—it was remote, out of the way, and she had three dogs so it was a good spot for her. I called her and she'd come tomorrow to pay for it and get the paperwork. Yay!

I drove back to the site with cardboard covered in plastic trash bags in the back of the Honda CRV; I loaded her used septic hose, cracked water hose, disgusting welcome mats, random batteries, and other crap.

As I dumped debris into the dumpster and tossed in my blue plastic gloves, I wondered if Bunny would show up for these belongings and accuse me of stealing.

I didn't care. Bunny, the amazing paranoiac, was off the property without me having to spend thousands on attorney's fees. Hopefully, fingers crossed, you will never hear about the new woman taking her spot, ever.

This was the best way to remove her from the property; if I had attorneys involved, she would have put up such a fight—that whole persecution and "everyone's after me" mentality would have cost me thousands. I'm sure she would have wanted a protracted trial before the judge and then the finale of sheriffs moving her out of the site just because we were all against her.

And Maris? She hoped the new lady tenant would be close to normal. And my hope for the new lady tenant? That she'd be okay with Maris.

Well, it turned out the problem *was* Maris after all.

Stay tuned for *that* fiasco, damn. It'll be in the second book.

PALATE CLEANSER

Low tide at the bay

I'M GOING TO HELL

The Smiths lived at the RV park for several months; they were quiet, peaceful, and pleasant people. They ended up moving out, and I wished them the best. If they ever wanted to come back, they'd be welcome.

Five months later, the Smiths drove in and asked if they could come back. I agreed and gave them an application, mostly for my records because I already knew they'd be great tenants.

About a week ago, Mrs. Smith called to check if there was an open site; I told her there would be one in a couple days. We made plans to coordinate their move onto the property and left it at that.

The site opened, and I called her on a Wednesday. She said she wanted the site and would organize the move.

I called her on Thursday for an update and left a message, but I didn't get a callback. No big deal, I knew she wanted the site.

I called her on Friday, left a message, and emailed her as well. No response. Hmm. Maybe they changed their minds? I've got a waiting list, and I was getting impatient.

On Saturday, I called and left a message stating that the site would go to another potential tenant if I didn't hear from her that day.

She called me Saturday afternoon… crying. She found her husband, Mr. Smith, dead on the floor Friday morning. It was sudden, and unexpected, obviously.

I apologized for being rude and gave her my condolences. She decided to move closer to her family for support.

I am the asshat.

PALATE CLEANSER

Butters

TUESDAY

I got a call at 7:00 in the morning from my tenant who was building me an additional chicken coop because those old broads, those entitled chickens, wouldn't share with the new young ones. Thus, there were two old asshole hens who wouldn't allow the new ten plus chicks to spend the night in their crib. Even the two roosters, who should have been hens, feared them.

It happens, no one says sexing chicks is 100% accurate. Thus, the two roosters I didn't want started crowing at 5:00 a.m. like dueling banjos but even more annoying. I knew this because they were usually outside my window.

And no, roosters are not necessary to get eggs.

Thus, the new henhouse was needed because I hated crawling through the goats' sleeping pens to retrieve eggs like it was some olde-timey pioneer egg hunt or finding random eggs scattered throughout the playground and gazebo.

But I digress. Back to the call. He said there was a homeless guy sitting on one of the nice chairs in front of the office. I jumped out of bed, jammed on a jacket and and went outside, calling 911 on the way. I should have put boots on, the concrete was freezing on my bare feet.

The young man, slumped over, looked lifeless as the tenant pushed his shoulder. The guy sat up, looked out of it, and finally creaked open his eyes. I asked him to leave the property since he was trespassing. His eyes slowly shut. I gave the 911 dispatcher a description of the guy and asked for an officer to get him off the property. This is all taking place in the dark, cold winter hours of early morning.

Homeless guy roused himself and yelled at me, going from sleep to rage in under five seconds. He said, "I get to stay here. I gave the camp host a propane tank, and he said I could."

Well, none of that was true because 1) the camp host is a woman; 2) camp host is a marine and would have kicked his ass to the curb. He was lucky she hadn't seen him.

I told dispatch that the guy was not leaving, and I needed help. While I waited and watched the guy leisurely stand, stretch, and gather his belongings, not going anywhere fast, the tenant waited with me. I appreciated the extra support.

We were again back to that theme. A woman telling a guy what to do just pissed him off.

Finally, he started off the property and I called 911 again and let them know he was headed south down the highway. A few minutes later, the officer drove in and stopped about fifteen feet from the covered porch.

I was in my pajamas, barefoot, and the puddles were ankle deep and it was storming hard. I gingerly tiptoed out on the sharp gravel and explained what happened. He handed me his card and told me to call the dispatch number and give all my pertinent information.

I told the officer that children waited here in front of the office for the school bus and that guy said he had a right to sleep here; I wanted him trespassed because he was going to come back. Once trespassed by the authorities, his return trip would buy him trouble.

He thought he could do what he wanted; after all, he bartered with the male manager this sweet sleep spot for a propane tank. It was highly likely I'd see him again.

Once inside, I called dispatch and gave my details. I spelled my first name, then my last name:

"S-P-R-I-N-G-E-R. Like in Jerry."

After a moment, dispatch guy laughed and asked, "Is Jerry still around?"

I replied, "Oh, sure, and probably hanging with my people."

He laughed harder, then asked, "Are you the manager or owner?"

I waited a beat and said, "Both, sir, both."

He added, "Well, if you see Jerry, tell him I said hi."

We shared a laugh. That was a good way to start a Tuesday.

P.S. A tenant said he saw the homeless sleepy guy on the property again. The tenant chased him off the property and as a parting gift smacked him upside the head. I did not ask him to do that. I also did not say that was a bad idea.

He said the guy had a machete hanging from his backpack. Well, that was a new development.

Damn, the doorbell just rang.

Anyway, thanks so much for your time and attention. I hope you enjoyed the outlandish tales of trailer park assholery.

Geez, again with the doorbell. Gotta go.

Thanks again. Take care. Stay safe.

Made in the USA
Columbia, SC
19 September 2022

67021351R00098